"You!" the Black Angel snarled as he raised his pistol

Calvin James swung his S&W subgun toward the mountain of black muscle who was intent on killing him. The Black Angel was no combat pro. He was still fumbling with the safety catch on his gun as James targeted on the Damballah snake charm hanging on the big man's chest and pulled the trigger.

Nothing happened.

The subgun had exhausted its magazine. James's fists tightened around the empty weapon. The Black Angel's broad face glowed as an evil smile swelled across his dark features.

"Looks like you rolled the dice again, brother," the Angel declared, aiming his pistol at James's face, "and lost!"

D1040773

Mack Bolan's
PHOENIX FORCE

PHOENIX FORCE

No Rules, No Referee

Gar Wilson

A GOLD EAGLE BOOK FROM

W🌐RLDWIDE

TORONTO · NEW YORK · LONDON · PARIS
AMSTERDAM · STOCKHOLM · HAMBURG
ATHENS · MILAN · TOKYO · SYDNEY

First edition March 1985

ISBN 0-373-61316-4

Special thanks and acknowledgment to
William Fieldhouse for his contributions to this work.

Printed in Canada

1

Congressman Walter Franklin was offended. He had arrived at the Nassau International Airport in New Providence and there was not a single television camera in sight. Just a handful of newspaper reporters. Franklin forced a smile and waved as two cameramen snapped their Nikons. The journalists opened their note pads and asked the standard questions without enthusiasm.

Franklin did not notice the small swarthy man dressed in a white linen suit and sunglasses. He stood apart from the reporters, discreetly photographing the congressman with a Simmons camera. The man took three pictures and quietly slipped away.

"Mr. Congressman," a reporter began, chewing a wad of gum as he spoke. "You've described this trip as a 'goodwill mission,' correct?"

"To improve relationships with the United States of America and her long-time island friends in the Bahamas," Franklin confirmed proudly.

"Uh-huh," the reporter said dryly. "Is there an urgent need for this trip? I mean, the Bahamas and the U.S. have always been on pretty good terms. . . ."

"I am not at liberty to discuss the details of my mission here," the congressman curtly replied.

"Excuse me, sir," a female reporter said. She had a British accent of some sort, but that did not mean she was with the London *Times*. A lot of people in the islands talked that way. "But will your mission, as you call it, be connected with the Bahamas Oil Refining Company in Freeport? Or is that 'for your eyes only,' as well?"

The other reporters chuckled at her remark. Franklin's smile became stiff, his facial muscles strained to keep the expression intact. Christ, he wanted to smack that smart-ass bitch in the mouth, but he kept grinning instead.

"Well," Franklin said with a halfhearted laugh. "I didn't mean to imply that I'm on a covert assignment for the CIA. It's just that I'll be discussing subjects of U.S. and Bahamian relations with the prime minister, and I'd rather not make a blanket statement until I've had a chance to talk with him. Okay?"

"Hey, Congressman," a cynical reporter said. He was dressed in a wrinkled tan suit and a cigarette dangled from his mouth. Franklin thought he looked as if he was rehearsing for the part of Mike Hammer. "You're a representative for a district in northeast Ohio, right? Mostly steel and auto workers live there, if I'm not mistaken."

"Grass-roots America," Franklin replied quickly. "Is there something wrong with that?"

"I just wonder how many of those grass-roots Americans can take a trip to the Bahamas in the middle of January."

"Your accent sounds like you're from New York," Franklin said stiffly. "But *you're* here, too."

"I'm from New Jersey," the reporter replied. "But my editors paid for my trip here—not the American taxpayers."

"I'm in Nassau on official business for the United States government," Franklin declared. "And I suggest you don't make absurd accusations in print unless your paper wants a lawsuit."

"I'm not accusing you of anything, Congressman," the newsman said with a shrug. "But I'd still like to know what connection a trip to the Bahamas has to representing auto and steel workers back in Ohio."

"I won't dignify that remark with a reply," Franklin declared as he strode past the reporters.

The congressman wanted to get away from the reporters. He had been disappointed that no TV people had been present, but now he was glad they had not been there to film his awkward response to the questions from those newspaper creeps. Who the hell did they think they were to talk to him that way? Trying to imply that he was taking a vacation in the Bahamas paid for by the American taxpayers. That was goddamn yellow journalism of the worst sort.

And so what if he was taking a vacation? Franklin did not see anything wrong with that. After all, he was a public servant. Franklin had a lot of responsibility. A congressman has to meet people all the time, and he has to vote on important legislation. Of course, Franklin only met with certain people, and he usually abstained from voting in Congress. Even a public servant cannot be expected to work all the time.

Franklin felt he deserved a vacation, anyway. He had given up a lucrative career as the head of a large law firm in Cleveland Heights when he entered the world of politics. Franklin actually took a cut in salary to become a public servant. Damn right, he was entitled to all the benefits, privileges and freebies he could get.

If a goodwill mission to the Bahamas happened to be one of his bennies, nobody should bitch. After all his sacrifices, Franklin figured he deserved a holiday, and he should not have to take a bunch of snotty crap from the press, either. What would those damn vultures do without politicians? They would have to rely on mass murderers, plane crashes and an occasional hotel fire for news, that's what.

Franklin spent half an hour stewing at the airport. He was even forced to get his own luggage and go through customs like everybody else. The congressman sat in the lobby by the airport entrance, sulking as he watched taxicabs and shuttle buses pass by. He still failed to notice the man in the white linen suit. The swarthy little fellow also sat in the lobby, leafing through a newspaper as if prepared to spend the entire day at the airport.

At last a pearl gray limousine arrived. The congressman struggled to repress his anger as he watched a chauffeur emerge from the vehicle to open the back door. Franklin's smile resembled a grimace of pain when he saw a tall white-haired stranger step from the limo. However, the man and his chauffeur recognized Franklin and headed toward him.

"You're not the prime minister," Franklin said with dismay.

"Indeed," the white-haired man admitted, extending a hand in greeting. "I'm Peter Sayers, deputy minister of tourism."

"Tourism?" Franklin replied, instinctively shaking hands with his professional politician's one-two-three arm pump. "But I'm a United States congressman...."

"And every year you make a goodwill trip to the Bahamas," Sayers sighed. "I know all about you, Congressman Franklin. Apparently, the PM feels that your trip falls under the category of VIP tourist."

"I'm not a goddamn tourist," Franklin snapped. "There must be a misunderstanding here, Mr. Sayers."

"Well, let's not have a scene in public," the deputy minister suggested. "Neither of us wants that. Why don't we talk in the car? If you're hungry, I know a nice sidewalk café on Meadow Street."

"I could do with some lunch," Franklin confessed. "I'll pick up the tab, of course. I can put it on the expense account."

"I'm sure," Sayers said dryly as he helped the chauffeur carry Franklin's baggage to the limo.

The swarthy little man in the white suit strolled to the closest telephone and fished two coins from his pocket.

THE GROTTO CAFE was pleasant and quaint. Congressman Franklin and Deputy Minister Sayers sat at a table beneath a large multicolored canopy. Franklin continued to ramble on about his burning desire to improve relations between the U.S. and the Bahamas. Sayers had listened to him for almost twenty minutes, and he still had no idea what the hell the congressman was talking about.

"Being with the ministry of tourism," Franklin said, "you might be interested in one of my ideas. Let's try to convince one of the airline companies to give a special discount to Bahamians who take a round-trip vacation to the United States. Especially trips to my home state."

"Ohio?" Sayers frowned. "Why would Bahamians want to go to Ohio?"

"Ohio is one of the greatest places in the United States," the congressman replied. "The tourists could arrive at the Cleveland Hopkins Airport and get to see one of the finest cities in the American Midwest. Cleveland is entirely different from Nassau, you know.''

"So I've heard," the deputy minister said as he nodded.

"In fact," Franklin continued, "as part of our efforts to promote goodwill, I will personally meet the first group of tourists who arrive at Cleveland. I'll show them Ohio. They'll get to see the factories, the shopping centers, Lake Erie and maybe Sea World. We've got one at Aurora, you know.''

"That's all very nice," Sayers began, "but the Bahamas wants to attract tourism to the islands. It's the main industry of our nation. We don't want to encourage people to go somewhere else.''

"It would be good public relations," Franklin insisted. "Goodwill for our countries.''

"Why don't you just enjoy your visit to the Bahamas?" the deputy minister urged. "Stop trying to convince us that you're here to champion any noble political causes.''

"I am insulted, sir!" Franklin exclaimed, his eyes wide, nostrils flared in an exaggerated expression of outrage. "I will tell the prime minister about your disrespect!''

"The prime minister does not wish to waste his time listening to another lazy American politician trying to disguise a vacation as a business trip. Save that charade for your voters, Mr. Congressman.''

"Am I to expect this sort of disrespectful treatment from everyone in the Bahamian government?" Franklin demanded.

"Certainly not," Sayers assured him. "I'll be happy to arrange for you to participate in tours to all the islands. Would you care for some brochures?''

"I think I can manage without them," Franklin glumly answered.

"Excuse me, gentlemen," the head waiter began as he approached the table. "There is a telephone call for Mr. Sayers. I am told it is from the prime minister himself."

"Thank you," Sayers replied. "Please excuse me, Mr. Congressman. Matters of state. I'm sure you understand."

"Of course," Franklin assured him.

Sayers briskly marched inside the restaurant while Congressman Franklin ordered another martini. Two men seated at a table nearby smiled as they sipped their iced tea. Both were suntanned and dressed in tennis outfits. The older man wore a straw hat and sunglasses. His younger companion had a visor with a green bill strapped to his tawny head.

No one paid much attention to the pair. They spoke softly. Occasionally the older man consulted his wristwatch. The blonde fiddled with a tennis racket. A casual observer would have seen nothing unusual about the pair, but a keen eye might have noticed one odd feature about them. Both men wore white gloves.

The elder one reached under the table for a blue airlines travel bag at his feet. He slipped a hand inside and groped about for a small metal box with a single plastic button in its center. The man nodded at his young friend. The blonde smiled thinly and reached for an identical bag under his chair. The senior man pressed the button.

A Volkswagen Rabbit parked at the curb across the street suddenly exploded. Metal and glass burst into flying debris as a great fireball erupted at the center of the vehicle. Naturally, all eyes turned toward the explosion.

Many customers at the Grotto Café jumped from their seats and bolted for cover, the two tennis players among them. The congressman remained seated, staring in horror at the burning wreckage across the street.

Franklin did not notice the blond man who quickly stepped behind him to thrust the blade of a diver's knife through the wicker backrest of the congressman's chair. Franklin's mouth opened in a small black oval as his body stiffened. He jerked weakly in a feeble muscular spasm. Then he fell forward, his face striking the rim of the table.

The two men in tennis clothing walked from the café. They moved at a steady pace, not too quickly. No one had paid much attention to them so far, and they did not want to attract any by running from the scene.

Congressman Franklin's body slid to the tiled floor of the patio. The knife was still lodged in the backrest of the chair, blood dripping from the long steel blade.

The congressman's vacation had come to an abrupt end.

2

Hal Brognola methodically chewed the cigar butt held between his teeth. He sat at the head of the conference table in the War Room and slowly gazed at the faces of the five men seated at the table.

Five very special men. The men of Phoenix Force, the most unusual antiterrorist commando team ever assembled.

Physically the five men had little in common. Colonel Yakov Katzenelenbogen, the unit commander of Phoenix Force, looked more like a college professor than a commando. Five foot ten, middle-aged and a bit overweight, Katz did not appear to be very menacing. Only the prosthesis attached to the stump of his right arm suggested Katz was experienced with violence.

Indeed, Katz had lots of experience. His warrior career had started as a teenager during the Nazi occupation of France. Most of the Katzenelenbogen family had been imprisoned in Hitler's concentration camps, but young Yakov joined the Resistance. A brilliant linguist, Katz already spoke French, Russian, German and English fluently. His skill with language and weapons and his natural talent for espionage did not go unnoticed by the American OSS who later enlisted him for behind-the-lines missions.

After the war, Katz joined the Haganah in Palestine

and participated in Israel's war for independence. When this goal was accomplished, Yakov enlisted in Mossad, Israel's primary intelligence organization. He fought in the Six Day War, in which his only son was killed by the same explosion that ruined his right arm beyond repair.

Although the damaged limb was amputated, Katz's spirit remained undefeated. He continued to carry out missions for Mossad and mastered Hebrew and Arabic to add to his linguistic skills. The CIA borrowed Katz for a couple of years, and the Israeli also served with the British SIS, the French Sûreté and the West German BND.

With an incredible background of experience in combat, espionage, counterintelligence and antiterrorism, Colonel Yakov Katzenelenbogen was the perfect choice as unit commander for Phoenix Force.

Gary Manning sat next to Katz. Twenty years younger than the Israeli colonel, Manning was a muscular, ruggedly handsome man. A former lieutenant in the Canadian army, he had served in the corps of engineers as a demolitions expert. Manning later served a tour in Vietnam as an observer, and spent more than a year attached to the Fifth Special Forces and the covert Special Operations Group. An exceptional rifleman, Manning operated as a sniper as well as an explosives expert. His skill and courage earned him the Silver Star for valor, and Manning was one of the very few Canadian citizens to receive this medal during the Vietnam era.

Manning returned to Canada, where he enlisted in the Royal Canadian Mounted Police. He was assigned to their newly formed antiterrorist division. Thanks to a special exchange program with West Germany, Manning spent 1971 to 1973 in Europe working with the elite

GSG-9 antiterrorist squad. He received a ton of experience in urban warfare as well as jungle combat.

A powerful man, the Canadian had seemingly inexhaustible reserves of strength and endurance, both mentally and physically. His bulldog determination made him strive to be the best at everything he attempted. More often than not he succeeded.

Gary Manning was certainly one of the best antiterrorists in the world, and so he was recruited for Phoenix Force.

Rafael Encizo leaned back in his chair and pared his nails with the blade of his Mark I Gerber fighting dagger. The Cuban warrior was good with a knife. He had learned to use a blade as a weapon in the streets of Havana even before he joined the freedom fighters pitted against Castro's regime. The Communists had slaughtered virtually all Encizo's family and forced young Rafael to flee to the United States in 1959.

Encizo was among the freedom fighters of the Bay of Pigs Invasion in 1961, where he was captured by the Communists and sent to El Principe, Castro's brutal political prison. Although he was beaten, starved and tortured, his spirit remained unbroken. The same cannot be said for a prison guard's neck after Encizo nearly twisted his head off in order to make his escape from El Principe.

The Cuban commando returned to the United States where he found various jobs that suited his unique skills. Encizo had been a scuba instructor, a treasure hunter and a professional bodyguard. He was working as an insurance investigator, specializing in maritime claims, when Phoenix Force recruited him to once again go to war against the enemies of civilization and freedom.

David McCarter was tired of sitting. He rose from his seat and began to pace the artillery-red carpet like a lion confined in a small cage. McCarter was a lion, more at home on the battlefield than in his native city of London.

The tall, fox-faced Briton was a veteran of the elite Special Air Service. He had seen action in Northern Ireland and during the Omani Ohofar War in Oman. McCarter had also been a special observer in Vietnam and he had the scars to prove it. The Briton also served as part of a clandestine "police action" in Hong Kong.

McCarter had been one of the SAS commandos to participate in Operation Nimrod, the successful siege on the Iranian embassy in London. An ace pilot and a pistol champion, McCarter was another ideal recruit for Phoenix Force.

Calvin James understood McCarter's restlessness, but he remained in his chair. The newest member of Phoenix Force did not want to appear impatient, although he was apprehensive about the meeting. It was the first time the group had been called to the War Room since Brognola chewed their asses for their unauthorized mission to England two months ago.

A tall, long-limbed black man, James was the only native-born American member of Phoenix Force, although Encizo was a naturalized U.S. citizen and Katz was preparing for final exams to dump his French citizenship and adopt dual Israeli-U.S. citizenship instead.

Calvin James was born and raised in the south side of Chicago. He grew up poor and he grew up tough, but he was a good athlete and a fast learner who vowed to use his considerable intelligence to get out of the goddamn ghetto and make something of himself.

At the age of seventeen, he joined the Navy and became a hospital corpsman with the elite SEAL (Sea, Air and Land) tactical unit. James was soon in Vietnam where he got his baptism of fire in jungle combat in Southeast Asia. He served with valor and distinction, receiving several decorations for his courage in the face of danger.

James returned to the States and continued to study for a career in medicine and chemistry on the GI bill. However, fate had marked out a different path for Calvin James. His mother and sister were both murdered by criminals. This incident convinced James to join the San Francisco Police Department. His combat skills and experience soon landed him a job with the SFPD Special Weapons and Tactics section, and although the SWAT team better suited his maverick personality, he never quite fitted in.

Then Phoenix Force drafted him to help deal with the insidious conspiracy of the Black Alchemist terrorists. Keio Ohara, one of the original Force members, was killed during that mission. The tall Japanese martial artist and electronics expert had been very popular with his teammates, and his loss was still a painful stab in the heart of every man at the table that day. However, Calvin James had proven himself to be worthy of Phoenix Force.

And that, he told himself, was something, because they were the best, the *very best* in the business.

No one knew this better than Hal Brognola. He was the control officer of Stony Man operations, the go-between for the President of the United States and a top-secret organization that had been created to combat the greatest threat to peace and freedom of the twentieth century—international terrorism.

Stony Man had originally been created to utilize the incredible combat skills of Mack Bolan, a warrior who had single-handedly battled the Mafia and driven the powers of organized crime into the ground. The Executioner had been the central figure of Stony Man. He personally selected the original five men for Phoenix Force to serve as a new American Foreign Legion.

Then fate threw Stony Man for a loss when Bolan was framed for a political assassination by the KGB. He became a fugitive and a renegade, stalked by virtually every intelligence and law-enforcement agency throughout the world. The Executioner was once again a lone wolf pitted against impossible odds.

Perhaps the President would have terminated the entire Stony Man operation if the sinister Black Alchemist conspiracy had not occurred shortly after Bolan's hasty departure from the organization. Phoenix Force crushed the terrorists and proved that Stony Man was still an effective weapon against the modern-day barbarians. And they had continued to prove it again and again.

"Well, you guys haven't been in the field for a couple of months," Brognola commented. "But you don't look like you've lost your edge."

"We've spent the last two months training," Katz replied. "Simulated desert combat in Arizona, forest environments in Canada, underwater demo and warfare off the Florida coast. Of course, you've seen our reports."

"About bloody time we got a real assignment," Mc-

Carter complained, still pacing like a father in a maternity waiting room.

"Yeah," Encizo added. "We had hoped you'd send us to Lebanon after that last terrorist bombing in Beirut."

"Maybe you would have been sent to Beirut," Brognola said dryly, "if you hadn't had that little adventure in London a while back."

"Aw, shit," Calvin James groaned. "You're not gonna bring that up again, Hal."

"That mission to England was totally unauthorized," the Fed stated. "I still haven't figured out how you managed that little miracle, but I have to admit it was a pretty good trick. You didn't get any help from British intelligence, the London police, the SAS or the Royal Marines, so God must have been on your side to successfully assault the Mardarajan embassy and get away without getting caught by the soldiers and cops surrounding the place."

"What's the difference?" Gary Manning said with a shrug. "It worked. We didn't blow our cover and we accomplished the mission without a hitch."

"But it could have been a disaster," Brognola insisted. "And the President guessed you guys were the five daredevils who attacked that embassy single-handed. Nobody else would be crazy enough to pull a stunt like that."

"Is that why we haven't been given a mission since we came back from England?" James asked.

"You guessed it," the Fed conceded.

"But what's the problem?" the black man began. "Everything went slicker than owlshit. The Mardarajan ambassador made a complete confession on live TV for the whole world to hear. He told all about the Libyan involvement and the SAS found plenty of evidence inside the embassy, as well. Colonel Khaddafi looks like a horse's ass and the British are happy with the outcome.''

"The point is the President of the United States gets a little worried when you guys run off to a foreign country to play Lone Ranger,'' Brognola explained. "After what happened with Colonel Phoenix, you can't blame him for being upset.''

"Colonel Phoenix was Mack Bolan,'' Manning commented. "We all knew that from the beginning, and there certainly isn't any point in playing that charade now.''

"Don't change the subject, Gary,'' the Fed told him. "That stunt in London was the second unauthorized mission you guys pulled. Did you tell Calvin about that business in Israel last year?''

"They told me,'' James confirmed.

"Did they also tell you the President was considering pulling the plug on Stony Man?''

"But he *didn't* pull the plug,'' Katz declared. "And he isn't going to. He needs us and he knows it.''

"Let's hope it stays that way,'' Brognola said. "Anyway, we've got a job for you guys. Wouldn't mind coming along on this one. At least I'd get away from the goddamn cold weather for a while.''

"Oh, boy,'' Encizo muttered. "Where are we going? El Salvador?''

"Nope,'' the Fed replied. "Not that far south. How does a trip to the Bahamas sound this time of year?''

"The Bahamas?'' Manning frowned. "What happened? Did some rich tourist lose his wallet and they're sending us to find it?"

"No," Brognola answered. "Yesterday a United States congressman lost his life in Nassau, but we don't expect you to recover it."

"Political assassination?" Katz inquired, taking a pack of Camel cigarettes from his pocket.

"That's what it looks like," the Fed confirmed as he leafed through a file folder. "Congressman Walter Franklin was murdered in the Grotto Café. Professional hit. Killers blew up a car to distract potential witnesses long enough for somebody to shove a shiv in Franklin's back. Blade was coated with garlic. That's an old gangster trick. If the wound doesn't kill your victim, the blood poisoning will. Hardly needed it in this case. The knife stabbed Franklin under the left shoulder blade up into the heart."

"How long was the blade?" Encizo, the knife artist, asked.

"About seven inches long," Brognola answered. "Diver's knife. No fingerprints on the weapon. Some of the witnesses think a couple of guys dressed in tennis outfits might be the killers, but nobody is sure. No one got a good enough look at them to give a decent description, anyway."

"What sort of explosives were used on the car?" Manning inquired.

"C-4 plastic explosives with a radio detonator," the Fed replied. "Like I said, professional all the way."

"According to this report," Katz began as he examined the file, "Franklin was having lunch with Deputy Minister Sayers of the Department of Tourism."

"That's right," Brognola nodded. "Less than a

minute before Franklin bought the farm, Sayers had gone into the restaurant to talk on the telephone with the P.M. The phone call was a phony, of course. Sayers was still in the building when all hell broke loose outside.''

"Clever," Manning remarked. "But it doesn't sound like a terrorist hit."

"I haven't finished yet," Brognola told him. "Franklin is the second U.S. citizen connected with the government to be assassinated in Nassau in the past two weeks. The first was a minor official from the U.S. Embassy, a diplomat named Fredrick Landers. He stepped out of a casino, started his car and it went boom. And guess what? Plastic explosives were used that time, too."

"Any idea who might be responsible?" Encizo asked.

"A group calling itself the Bahamians Against Capitalist Oppression is taking credit for both murders," Brognola stated. "Apparently BACO doesn't like Americans."

"I never heard of BACO before," Katz said with a frown. The Israeli had a mind like a computer with memory banks full of data about espionage, intelligence and terrorist activity. "Must be something new."

"I've never heard of it either," Encizo added. "Does Bear have anything on BACO?"

Aaron Kurtzman was Bear, Stony Man's resident computer wizard. Kurtzman had been crippled for life by a bullet he took in the spine during a siege on Stony Man headquarters. Although confined to a wheelchair, Bear still handled a console like a superchamp. Aaron Kurtzman fit right in at Stony Man. Nothing could break him and he never gave up.

"No, he hasn't," Brognola answered. "We figure it's

some sort of Pro-Castro group. Probably has its roots in Havana. You guys can tell us all about them after you stomp the shit out of the bastards.''

"Doesn't sound like much of a mission," McCarter said as he frowned. "Probably just a tiny group of would-be revolutionaries. Bahamian version of the Baader-Meinhof gang. Wouldn't be surprised if the local authorities have the whole thing wrapped up by now.''

"Unless the terrorists have moved from New Providence to one of the other islands," Encizo remarked. "They may even head for Cuba.''

"The President wants you to take care of this mission," Brognola told them. "He doesn't want you to go to Lebanon and blow the hell out of every Palestinian terrorist operating in Beirut. He doesn't want you in El Salvador. This might not be the biggest assignment Phoenix Force has ever had, but at least you guys won't wind up on the six o'clock news. Any questions?''

"Just one," Katz replied. "I've studied this folder and I didn't find anything to suggest there were any victims besides Franklin and Landers.''

"Don't sound so disappointed," the Fed commented. "Do you want higher body counts, Yakov?''

"I don't," the Israeli assured him. "But most terrorists would. This BACO outfit seems to have made an effort to be certain they didn't kill any innocent bystanders. That's very considerate for a terrorist group.''

"BACO is a new outfit," McCarter commented. "Maybe they don't know the rules yet.''

"Will we have a contact in the Bahamas?" Manning asked Brognola.

"Yeah," the Fed answered, leafing through his notes.

"The Bahamian Security Intelligence Service will assist you. One of their case officers will meet you at the airport in Nassau. Get this—his name is Maj. Pendexter Alby."

"Well, one thing about Phoenix Force," Calvin James commented as he grinned, "we get to go to exotic places and meet interesting people with funny names. Besides, how can you beat a job that gives you an all-expense paid trip to the Bahamas, man."

"This mission might sound easy," Katz began. "But we're not going on a holiday. Anyone who'll murder a U.S. congressman in a public place in broad daylight shouldn't be taken lightly."

"You sure know how to give a pep talk, Yakov," James said sourly.

3

Don Antonio Fazzio held the white mouse by its tail and dangled it over the glass lid of the seventy-five gallon aquarium. The don opened the lid and dropped the hapless rodent into the water. Fazzio stepped back and watched the mouse struggle. The tiny beast swam pretty well, keeping its snout above water as its feet paddled rapidly to stay afloat. The mouse slid its nose along the glass side panel of the aquarium and squealed fearfully.

"Dinner is served," Fazzio whispered with a cruel smile.

He watched the fish move toward the mouse, attracted by the animal's motion. Twelve large piranha rapidly advanced, mouths open to reveal columns of needlelike teeth. Fazzio watched the fish attack. He never failed to marvel at the savage ruthlessness of the piranha. The fish swiftly seized the mouse and pulled it down, a dozen jaws biting and tearing in unison.

Blood seeped from rent flesh. It formed a dark cloud in the water. The scent drove the piranha into a violent feeding frenzy. They ripped flesh, hastily gulping chunks of meat and immediately biting again and again. Fazzio could see little except the thrashing bodies of the hungry fish and some mangled remnants of meat and bone that slowly sank to the gravel bottom of the tank.

Fazzio understood the piranha. Their world was not

unlike his own. Greed and ambition drove men as the feeding frenzy motivated the piranha. Attack quickly without mercy and grab the biggest chunk you can. Gulp it down and go back for more. If you don't do it, somebody else will. Gobble it up fast and leave nothing behind but a well-chewed skeleton.

You have to become bigger and stronger than the other fish. Fazzio once had twice as many piranha in that tank. The big ate the little. This was something else the don knew about. Cannibalism was practiced in his world, as well.

Fazzio had been born and bred to *La Cosa Nostra*. His father had been a mafioso and his father before him. Fazzio's family had been connected since his ancestors moved from Sicily to the Land of Opportunity to become muscle for a Black Hand protection racket in New York's "Little Italy" in 1912.

The mob was a way of life for the Fazzio family. However, Antonio had been the first of his bloodline to achieve the honored title of capo. He was forty-one years old and in the prime of life. Fazzio remained fit and strong by careful diet and regular exercise. He swam every day in his kidney-shaped pool and once or twice a week he would head for the coast and go spear-fishing in the Atlantic. Once a hammerhead shark had attacked the don. Fazzio's men still recall how Fazzio had emerged from the water dragging the six-foot-long killer fish to the shore. The shark's belly was ripped open and Fazzio's knife still jutted from the side of the fish's head, the blade buried deep in an eye socket.

The don was a big fish now. Bigger and meaner than any son of a bitch in his territory.

But it had been a long hard road to power. Fazzio had

started out as a common gunsel for Don DiGiorgio, who traded him to a fledgling capo named Ciro Lavangetta in Arizona. Traded him like a goddamn football player in the NFL. After DiGiorgio died, it looked as if the Lavangetta family was going to become a major power in the *commissione* after the "Council of Kings" was held in Miami. The big piranha would surface and the little fish would fall into place behind them.

Then the shark came to town. Not a hammerhead that could be taken out with a knife, but a great white shark. A goddamn killer whale that called itself the Executioner.

A sleek predator dressed in black combat uniform and armed with an arsenal of ultradeadly weaponry, Mack Bolan hit Miami. Hard. The Executioner used military tactics and awesome firepower to assault the Council of Kings. Mafia buttonmen were no match for Bolan's super weapons and superb combat skill. Fazzio had been one of the very few mafioso to survive the violent encounter.

After the massacre, Fazzio moved from family to family until he became a hitter for Max Spielke in Acapulco. Spielke was Jewish and could never be a true don. But he was given the honorary title of capo *Mexicano* because he was in charge of *La Cosa Nostra* operations in Acapulco. It promised to be a bold new world, another success story for the monarchs of organized crime.

And then the shark returned.

The Executioner hit the Acapulco organization like a bolt of killer lightning. Spielke was killed. So were most of his soldiers. Once again, Fazzio had been lucky. He was a rarity, a Mafia hardcase who had survived two Bolan attacks.

Fazzio still had nightmares about those days. The Executioner was more than a madman with a fancy array of sophisticated weapons, more than a highly trained professional fighting man. Bolan had been an indestructible force that could strike anywhere, anytime.

To some people, the Executioner became some sort of hero. Robin Hood with a gun, Saint George taking on the Mafia dragon. But the mob regarded Bolan as an evil spirit, a deadly shadow that lurked in every corner. The Executioner was a vengeful Zeus with high-velocity lightning and explosive thunder.

Nonetheless, the Executioner was a nightmare of the past. Mack Bolan had been killed in a final gun battle years ago. There had been rumors that the Executioner was still alive, but Fazzio figured that was bullshit propaganda put out by the Feds. Hell, some people claim Adolf Hitler and James Dean are still alive, too.

Sure, a few criminal operations that involved veterans of the mob had been wrecked by somebody who used tactics similar to Bolan's, but there had not been a verified Executioner assault for more than three years. The remnants of the Mafia had spent that time lying low, licking their collective wounds like a sick hydra. It was time to come out of hiding. Time to return to *La Cosa Nostra*—"this thing of ours."

However, the mob had been severely damaged by Bolan the Bastard. It lacked its former strength and manpower. The Executioner wars had left the Mafia crippled and fragmented. But, the czars of organized crime were businessmen and long ago learned the value of merging with other family forces in order to form a more powerful whole unit.

Perhaps Fazzio should have thanked the Executioner.

He never would have risen to the rank of capo if the mob had not been torn asunder by Bolan and virtually all the big bosses slain. Yet Fazzio was not terribly thankful for his new partners in crime. He fatalistically accepted this. After all, business is business.

"Don Fazzio," Henri LeTrec began. "If you have finished feeding your pets, we are ready to begin the conference."

LeTrec was a few years younger than Fazzio, but his belly was soft and he sported a triple chin. The don guessed he was too fond of French pastries. However, LeTrec's eyes had the cold hard quality of ruthlessness that labeled him as a big piranha with the potential to become even larger in the future.

Fazzio did not like LeTrec's nasal voice, but he figured all Frenchmen talked that way. Still, the don was forced to admire the Frenchy's linguistic ability. LeTrec spoke both English and Italian fluently and he treated the capo with proper, if less than sincere, respect.

Of course, Henri LeTrec was a Corsican by birth. A member of the Union de Corse—the Corsican Syndicate—LeTrec was accustomed to the protocol and traditions of the family. Although the Union de Corse is technically separate from the Mafia, the two criminal societies are very similar and frequently cooperated to achieve common goals.

The Corsican smiled thinly as he watched the piranha devour the mouse. LeTrec did not find pleasure in the savagery of the killer fish. He was amused by Don Fazzio's choice of entertainment. The piranha were obviously a subtle warning to the other members of MERGE. This was the capo's territory and anyone who displeased Don Fazzio could wind up as food for the fish.

The don sat at the head of the conference table. He noticed the sly smile on LeTrec's round face, then his gaze shifted to Juan Vargas, a kingpin from the so-called "Mexican Mafia." Vargas watched the piranha, his eyes ablaze with cruel delight. The Mexican hoodlum had always loved the bullfights and cockfights in his native land. He did not appreciate the skill and courage of the matador or the competition of betting on the dueling roosters. Vargas enjoyed the violence and bloodshed, the excitement of watching one living creature destroy another.

Raul Ortega sat across from Vargas. He clucked his tongue with disgust at the Mexican's display of blood-lust. Vargas was acting like a sex maniac who found a peephole to the girls' shower. Ortega had barely glanced over his shoulder at the feeding piranha. The fish neither repulsed nor excited him. He really did not care what kind of pets Don Fazzio kept at his home.

A high-ranking member of the Colombian Syndicate, Ortega had seen countless killings and tortures. He had been involved in the production of "snuff movies" in the late 1960s. Young women, usually un-suspecting prostitutes, were murdered in front of a camera simply to film a sick novelty item for a sadistic market.

Ortega had watched syndicate pimps beat and torture prostitutes who failed to make enough money hustling in the streets of Bogotá. He had witnessed the brutal maiming and murder of junkies and their families when addicts did not pay syndicate dealers on time. Ortega had participated in numerous acts of violence, including the executions of three lieutenants who turned against the syndicate.

Raul Ortega was immune to the horror of violence, but he was still uncomfortable with the other members of MERGE. Don Fazzio and Henri LeTrec represented the only truly international sections of the organization. The Mafia and the Corsican Syndicate were far more sophisticated and powerful than the Colombian criminal network—and everybody in the room knew it. Juan Vargas and his Mexican hoodlums were brutes with a street-gang mentality. They were too concerned with machismo nonsense to be truly cunning or reliable in an emergency that required more than physical bravado. The fifth man at the table, Paul Wainwright, was a coward. He was the weakest link in the Bahamian operation and would have to be watched most carefully.

Wainwright was the only native-born Bahamian at the conference table. A thirty-six-year-old Caucasian of British descent, he had turned away when he saw Don Fazzio drop the mouse in the piranha tank. Wainwright's face became chalky white and he began sweating, despite the air conditioner.

Don Fazzio tapped a silver spoon against the side of his crystal tumbler of iced tea to call the meeting to order.

"Well, gentlemen," he began. "We all know the reason for this conference. Let us dispense with the minutes of our last meeting. Mr. LeTrec, I believe you have some good news for us. Correct?"

"*Oui*, Don Fazzio," the man said, nodding. "As you know, my colleagues in France process and distribute heroin in large quantities. Thanks to Mr. Wainwright's connections with one of the Bahamian stevedore unions, we'll be receiving a shipment of approximately two hundred kilos of heroin the day after tomorrow.''

"Further distribution of these narcotics will be in the hands of Señor Vargas and Señor Ortega," the don declared. "Gentlemen?"

"The sources of the Mexican mafia, as my *companeros* call the organization," Vargas began with a smile, "include distribution throughout Mexico and the southwestern United States. We've been dealing marijuana and certain other drugs, including some heroin, in this region for many years. An increase of our supply of heroin will indeed be welcome, Don Fazzio."

"Just remember you and your 'Mafia' are now part of MERGE," Fazzio said coolly. "Don't forget your partners, amigo."

"Don't you worry about that," Vargas assured him. "We all have the same interests, so it benefits us to cooperate, no?"

"*Mejicanos* have never been noted for cooperation," Ortega sneered.

"Let's not stir up a hornets' nest," Fazzio said quickly before Vargas could reply to the Colombian's remark. "What about your syndicate connections, *señor*?"

"As you know," Ortega began, fitting a cigarette in a long black-and-gold holder. "The Colombian syndicate extends from the northern part of South America into most of Central America and virtually all of the United States. Of course, our main commodity is cocaine. This is a very popular narcotic these days. We have almost thirty million customers in the United States alone. Many of these never free-base cocaine, but a large number will surely be interested in graduating from coke to heroin. In some cases, we may be able to introduce the drug without the customer's knowledge.''

''But your syndicate can assure us of a large profit, correct?'' Fazzio asked.

''Approximately six hundred million dollars a year,'' Ortega replied. ''That's the projected combined profits of our regular cocaine market plus the probable heroin sales.''

''Excuse me, Don Fazzio,'' LeTrec began. ''But have you been able to secure our proposed bank account in Grand Cayman? As I understand it, the banking structure there will be perfect for us. Revealing confidential information about accounts or safe deposits is a felony in Cayman, punishable by two years in prison. This promises to assure us ideal security for our profits.''

''I've spoken with Don Mancini about Cayman,'' Fazzio replied. ''And he feels that our accounts should remain in Switzerland for the time being. The Caymanian banking system is no longer ideal for our purposes. The United States Narcotics Department has suspected someone might take advantage of the Cayman's banking system, and the Americans and the British have joined forces to pressure the Caymanian government into permitting investigations of certain 'suspicious accounts.' ''

''Invasion of privacy,'' LeTrec muttered with a frown. ''How unsporting of them.''

''That leaves us with only one matter to discuss,'' Fazzio began. ''The assassination of a certain United States congressman. Perhaps you'd care to explain this, Señor Ortega?''

''I didn't try to hide the fact I had Congressman

Franklin killed," Ortega replied as he shrugged. "And I already told you why it had to be done. My best people handled the job. The police don't have a single clue except that the Bahamians Against Capitalist Oppression are taking credit for the assassination. This, of course, will lead them nowhere."

"This isn't El Salvador or Argentina," Paul Wainwright stated, mopping his brow with a linen handkerchief. "You can't go about murdering people in Nassau and expect everyone to just look the other way. Let alone killing a bloody congressman from the States."

"And you don't know everything involved in this incident," Ortega replied simply.

"Last week you told us why you had to kill a U.S. diplomat," Wainwright snapped. "Now you're going to tell us that the Americans won't care about the murder of this congressman? We're going to wind up with the goddamn CIA in Nassau."

"The CIA is a joke," Juan Vargas grunted. "Nobody worries about them anymore. They don't have any *cajónes*. The gringo spies won't do a thing about nothin'."

"The situation will work itself out," Ortega assured the others. "You'll see. No one will do anything about it. No one will *want* to do anything."

"I certainly hope you're right," Fazzio commented. "Because if you are not, we'll have no choice about what we can do about the situation. To be blunt, Mr. Ortega, you will be our scapegoat. We'll throw you to the wolves and let you take full blame for the whole business."

"It will all work out fine, Don Fazzio," the Colombian insisted, but his voice did not sound quite so confident when he repeated the claim.

"Well, what's done is done," the don sighed. "Back to the other matters of business, gentlemen."

4

Phoenix Force arrived at the International Airport in Nassau. They barely had time to step off the plane when Maj. Pendexter Alby approached the commandos. He had no trouble recognizing the five men based on the descriptions he received at SIS headquarters.

Phoenix Force recognized Alby from a photograph and description given to them at Stony Man headquarters. The major was a large black man, heavily built, with a large face and a heavy lantern jaw. Sunlight flashed against the thick lenses of his horn-rimmed glasses as he gazed up at the five warriors.

"Welcome to the Bahamas," Alby greeted, but his ebony features were stern and his voice was cold and formal.

"A pleasure to meet you, Major," Yakov Katzenelenbogen replied, extending his left hand. The three steel hooks of his prosthesis were clamped around the handle of a briefcase. The artificial hand resembled the talons of a bird of prey.

"I'm sure," Alby said grimly. He ignored Katz's hand. "Shall we talk in the office, gentlemen?"

"We have a rather special crate among our luggage," Katz told him. "We need to get it first."

"That's already been covered with customs," Alby assured him. "Although I'm surprised you didn't simply use diplomatic immunity. That's how the CIA usually gets equipment into the country, isn't it?''

"That's also how a lot of people get their first clue that somebody is with the CIA," David McCarter said dryly. "Standing around in this airport talking about confidential matters is just about as stupid, but since you started this bloody—''

"Let's just get our gear and talk later," Katz urged, cutting off the sharp-tongued Briton as quickly as possible.

"Very well," Alby agreed. "I'm using the office of the airport security right now.''

"Oh, bloody hell," McCarter groaned.

"That is inadequate security, Major," Katz told him. "I suggest we load our luggage into a shuttle bus and head for the Atlantis hotel.''

"What's wrong with the office here?" the major asked, clearly annoyed.

"We'll discuss that subject later, Major," the Israeli answered curtly.

"By what authority are you giving me orders, sir?" Major Alby demanded.

"It should have been made clear to you that our authority comes from the President of the United States and the office of the governor general of the Bahamas," Katz replied. "If you don't believe us, please check with your superiors. If you can't accept the fact that we're in charge of this assignment, then you'll be replaced by someone more cooperative.''

"We'll discuss this matter in more detail when you're satisfied with security, sir," Alby said stiffly. "I wouldn't want to make you chaps unhappy.''

"You've been all smiles and sunshine so far, man," Calvin James commented with a shrug.

Phoenix Force loaded their luggage, including a large wooden crate, into a shuttle bus. Major Alby showed the driver an ID card for the Ministry of Transport and Civil Aviation and told the man not to take any more passengers. All six men climbed into the vehicle and the bus pulled away from the curb.

"All right, Major," Katz began in a low voice. "Now, I'll explain why the airport isn't secure. Congressman Franklin arrived at the airport and Deputy Minister Sayers met him. Both men left in a limo and headed for a restaurant that was apparently chosen at random. This means the killers must have had a lookout posted at the airport in order to know which vehicle to follow. The assassins then tailed the limo to the Grotto Café and carried out their scheme to kill Franklin."

"And you're claiming that the BACO terrorists group is sophisticated enough to carry out this plot?" Alby scoffed. "The SIS and the Nassau police have investigated the murders of both Congressman Franklin and Fred Landers, and we don't have a single solid clue. We haven't found a shred of evidence to suggest this Bahamians Against Capitalist Oppression ever existed."

"Except for two dead American citizens," Gary Manning commented. "What do you call that, Major?"

"I call it annoying," Alby said with a shrug.

"That's an odd way to describe murder," Katz remarked, raising his eyebrows with surprise.

"What else can one say about two murders that aren't *supposed* to be solved?" the SIS man replied.

"You're being real cute, Major," James said sharply. "Why don't you quit playing games and say what's on your mind?"

"When one investigates a murder," Alby began,

"one looks for a motive. Now who had something to gain by killing Franklin and Landers?"

"What is this?" McCarter growled. "A bleedin' quiz show?"

"Look," the major said crossly, "the Bahamian Security Intelligence Service may not be as large as the CIA or NATO Intelligence or whatever you blokes are associated with, but we still have considerable resources of information within the Bahama islands."

"That's great news," Encizo said dryly. "And what earth-shaking information did you come up with?"

"Something you're probably already aware of, I'm sure," Alby replied. "Fred Landers was being investigated by the Nassau police, the U.S. Narcotics Department and, no doubt, the CIA, for the last four months. It seems Mr. Landers liked to gamble at the Neptune's Palace, a casino on East Bay Street."

"That's legal in Nassau, isn't it?" Manning inquired.

"Gambling isn't against the law," Alby confirmed. "But the use of cocaine is."

"Cocaine?" Katz cocked his head to one side. "You're saying that Landers was an addict?"

"Almost certainly," the SIS officer confirmed. "Landers was frequently seen in the company of a notorious criminal known as the 'Black Angel.' This villain is suspected of running a loan-shark operation in Nassau, and he's probably trafficking in cocaine, as well. He's a great bloody brute, but he's clever. The police can't prove the Angel is guilty of anything worse than having a bad tailor."

"What about Congressman Franklin?" Katz asked.

"Come now," Alby sighed. "You know as well as I do that Franklin was under a congressional investigation even before he left the States. He was suspected of a number of acts of misconduct, including misuse of government funds, taking sexual liberties with certain female members of his staff and indulging in the use of illegal narcotics.''

''Cocaine?'' Encizo asked.

''Probably marijuana, as well,'' the major said. ''Or perhaps Quaaludes. Cocaine freaks often use such drugs to take the edge off their coke high since cocaine is a stimulant and the others are depressants.''

''They use alcohol, too,'' James added. ''Booze will take the edge off just as much as pot or 'ludes. . . which isn't enough to keep a coke freak from going from bad to worse. A lot of cocaine users become alcoholics, as well, because they try to balance out their high. Dumb bastards.''

''Let's save the discussion on drug abuse for a tea party,'' McCarter commented gruffly. ''What I want to know is whether any of this has a goddamn thing to do with the BACO terrorists or why Franklin and Landers were murdered.''

''I think it's quite obvious why they were murdered,'' Alby replied simply. ''Landers and Franklin were an embarrassment to the United States government. So Washington took care of it in a direct and ruthless manner.''

''My God.'' Manning glared at Alby. ''You think the CIA did it.''

''That's right,'' the major admitted. ''And I don't give a damn if you blokes are with the Company or not. The bloody CIA does a lot of dirty work in Bermuda and the Bahamas. It's the closest safe house they can have in order to carry out operations in the Caribbean concerning Castro.''

"Jamaica is closer to Cuba than the Bahamas," Encizo remarked with a shrug. "But I don't think this changes your mind about the CIA."

"The Company killed Landers and Franklin," Alby insisted. "And they fabricated this so-called BACO terrorist organization in order to throw the authorities off the track. The mythical BACO group will be blamed for the assassinations and those two cocaine-sniffing lice will become martyrs killed in the war against international terrorism."

"And why do you think we're here?" James asked.

"You're part of the smoke screen," the major explained. "Washington sent you to conduct a false investigation to give the impression this BACO group is genuine. You'll go through all the motions, pretend to be looking for these fictional terrorists, and then you'll go home and file your reports. Washington will tell the world how they tried to find the assassins, but the terrorists got away—because of the carelessness of the Bahamian authorities, of course."

"Wait a bloody minute. . . ." McCarter began angrily.

"Relax, Mr. Daniels," Katz urged, calling the Briton by his cover name. "The major is merely stating his opinion. We know he's wrong, but Major Alby still doubts our motives. Getting angry with him won't change his opinion."

"I hope the major realizes if the United States is responsible for these assassinations," Manning began, "that also means the Bahamian government must have cooperated with this 'CIA cover-up' in order to make this so-called conspiracy a success."

"It wouldn't surprise me if the United States managed to bully my government into agreeing to this business," Alby replied. "After all, the U.S. virtually runs our oil industry. Tourism is our number-one money maker, and the bulk of our tourist trade is from the States. Banking is our second largest industry, and most of our major clients are either from the United States or Western Europe. It is a sad fact, but the Bahamas is indeed dependent on outside influences. My government may have been forced to cooperate with Washington."

"How very paranoid," Katz mused. "What if your theory is wrong, Major? What if the BACO terrorists are real and the CIA isn't responsible for the murders?"

"Can you prove I'm wrong?" Alby insisted.

"You can't prove you're right," Calvin James declared. "We're here to find out who's responsible for those assassinations. Are you going to help us or do we have to get somebody else?"

"What do you want?" Alby inquired.

"You can start by getting us copies of the information you have on Franklin, Landers and this Black Angel character," Katz replied. "We'd also like firearms permits to carry concealed weapons in the Bahamas."

"The prime minister's office has already authorized that," the major said as he nodded. "In fact, you've been authorized to carry full-automatic weapons. I'm surprised that such firepower has been approved for five foreigners."

"Some people just like to do those sorts of things for us," Encizo said with a smile. "Sure makes it easier for us to do our job that way."

"What's in that crate?" Alby asked. "You five certainly didn't bring enough firearms and ammunition to fill it."

"We didn't?" McCarter grinned. "What do you think we have in there? A set of filing cabinets?"

"Well," Alby began awkwardly, "what do you intend to do with all that weaponry?"

"We take it with us all the time," James said with a shrug. "And somehow we always manage to find a use for that stuff."

"I'm beginning to wonder what you people are going to do while you're in the Bahamas," Major Alby remarked, a trace of apprehension in his voice.

"Hang around," Katz suggested. "Maybe you'll find out."

5

Nassau is the capital of the Bahamas. It has been a Disneyland for jet-setters since the Duke and Duchess of Windsor chose to reside in Nassau during the 1940s. Yet the biggest New Year's celebration is the Junkanoo festival that originated with African slaves brought to the islands. The Bahamas has a black majority, and many of the old settlements were founded by freed slaves.

New Providence was a British colony in 1656, and the old English influence is still found in Nassau. The Bahamas is the land of the buccaneers. It was the home of Blackbeard and Calico Jack. Now Providence is rich in history and brimming with glamour and excitement. And Nassau is the crown jewel of the Bahamas.

East Bay Street is best known for its delightful shops and stores, the Savile Row of the Bahamas. The Neptune's Palace was a gaudy concrete hulk among the quaint collections of shops. A clapboard figure with a white beard, pointed crown and trident in hand was mounted above the porch roof. It would have been more appropriate at the entrance of a funhouse than a casino.

"I told you blokes you were overdressed," Lieutenant Steward remarked as he wheeled the black Mercedes into the casino parking lot. "The Neptune's Palace isn't exactly Blades, you know."

"We sure know it now," Calvin James muttered, carefully buttoning his white dinner jacket and checking the bulge of the .45-caliber Colt Combat Commander under his left armpit. "We should have worn bowling shirts and sneakers, man."

"Doesn't hurt us to dress up once in a while," Rafael Encizo remarked. The Cuban was confident that his black tuxedo jacket concealed a compact Walther PPK in shoulder leather and his pet Mark I Gerber fighting dagger clipped at the small of his back.

"I feel like a bloody headwaiter," David McCarter complained. He also wore a tux, the jacket a size too large for his tall, lean frame. Fashion never mattered much to the British commando. He was more concerned that the jacket covered his 9mm Browning autoloader and Bianchi shoulder rig. McCarter also wore a .38 Smith & Wesson Airweight in a clip holster on his belt.

"You've seen the Black Angel in this place before, Lieutenant?" James asked their driver.

"A number of times," Steward confirmed grimly. "The Angel's real name is Percy Haldren. You can't miss the bastard. Big man. Very big. Haldren's built like a bloody ox, but he's a very flashy dresser. Always wears a gold earring in his left earlobe and a medallion around his neck."

"With a snake emblem in the center," Encizo commented. "That was mentioned in his file. It represents the voodoo god Damballah, right?"

"That's right," Steward confirmed. "Haldren was born in the Bahamas, but he spent some time with the Ton Ton Macout in Haiti. That's what they call their secret police. Named them after some sort of voodoo boogeymen who kidnap children. Goddamn brutes. Mean as hell and totally ruthless."

"So I've heard," James commented. He did not tell Steward that Phoenix Force had clashed with a terrorist network known as the Black Alchemists that was largely comprised of former Ton Ton Macout. "Everybody know the game plan for tonight?"

"Not too complicated," McCarter replied. "You and I are going to lose a lot of money in the casino and hope we can get the Black Angel to offer us a loan."

"And Steward and I will be around to back you up if you need any help," Encizo added.

"I've always been able to lose money without any assistance," the Briton said with a shrug.

The plan was simple, but it was a long shot and they all knew it. The Black Angel might not be at the casino or he might ignore the bait. Even if the loan shark took an interest in McCarter or James, it was unlikely he would attempt to approach either man the first night.

They were lucky to have Lieutenant John Steward with them. The SIS officer had formerly been a Nassau policeman, a vice cop familiar with local underworld characters. Steward knew the city and he knew the major criminals that inhabited it.

When Major Alby assigned Steward to assist Phoenix Force, it had been his first effort to cooperate with the commando team. While James, Encizo and McCarter pursued one possible lead, Katz, Manning and Alby were checking other sources of information. But there were no guarantees that any would be successful.

The three Phoenix Force warriors and Lieutenant Steward walked to the Neptune's Palace casino and mounted the stairs. A doorman dressed in a colorful red-and-gold uniform politely welcomed them.

Inside, the casino was full of flash and glitter.

Chandeliers of ornate glass, designed to resemble crystal, hung from the ceilings. The carpets were bright red, and mirrors covered most of the walls.

"Half those mirrors are one-way glass," Steward informed the others in a quiet voice. "The casino is always watching for cheats and thieves."

"Does the casino cheat?" James asked.

"I'm not sure if the Neptune's Palace does or not," Steward replied. "But most casinos don't cheat. They don't have to because enough people lose enough money to assure them of a profit. Besides, the gambling commission watches all the casinos for corruption and they'll pull the owners' license if they catch the house cheating customers."

"This place doesn't seem to attract too many customers," Encizo remarked as he scanned the groups of people clustered around the gambling tables.

"Neptune's Palace isn't a very large casino," Steward explained. "As you can see, it doesn't have as much to offer gamblers as the larger houses."

Indeed, the Neptune appeared to have only four choices for games of chance—roulette, baccarat, blackjack and craps. One could almost separate the American and European tourists by the games they selected. The former favored the blackjack and craps tables while the latter preferred baccarat and roulette.

Steward was right about the casino being far from a black-tie environment. The dealers wore short-sleeve shirts open at the throat. Many of the players were also clad in casual attire, especially Americans accustomed to the fun-city atmosphere of Las Vegas. The Europeans, familiar with the formal setting of Monte Carlo and Porto Karras, tended to overdress for the Neptune.

The Phoenix Force trio was grateful for this because they would have attracted unwanted attention if no one else in the casino wore a tuxedo or dinner jacket.

Calvin James and David McCarter headed for the cashier cage to get chips. Encizo and Steward moved to a bar where they could watch the casino without being obvious. Manning took his chips to the baccarat table while James joined a craps game.

The Briton took a chair next to a heavyset gray-haired woman who gave McCarter a look of disdain when she noticed how poorly his jacket fit. Manning grinned at her and winked suggestively. The woman decided to play roulette as the dealer began the auction to determine who would be the banker.

"Banco," Manning announced.

The shoe was passed. Manning started the bet at three hundred dollars. Several players passed. About half accepted. The Briton dealt the first hand. Manning got a two of hearts and a two of spades.

"I vish to raise bet, *Mein Herr*," a middle-aged player with a thick Bavarian accent declared. "Five hundred American dollars. *Es ist gut, ja?*"

"Fine with me," McCarter agreed. "Anybody else?"

The rest passed. The Briton dealt the second hand.

"Eight," the German said with a smile, displaying his cards.

"Nine," McCarter read his total, surprised when he drew a five.

"Congratulations," the German said. "You must be lucky tonight, *Mein Herr*."

"Yeah," McCarter replied glumly. "Let's try again and see what happens."

Calvin James had better luck losing at the crap table.

He had never cared much for gambling and could not understand how people could enjoy risking their money on anything as chancy as the turn of a card or the roll of dice. James had worked his way up from the ghetto and he knew the value of money. He appreciated it too much to take such risks.

Being a chemist as well as a commando and the unit medic, James was a good mathematician, and he knew something about the odds of winning or losing certain rolls of the dice. He also knew that the odds increase in favor of the house because of restrictions placed on crap games in most casinos.

"Ten the hard way," he announced, rattling a pair of dice in a cup. "Any takers?"

"You got one here, son," a rawboned fellow with a Texas accent and a gray Stetson perched on his head replied.

"Okay." James spoke to the dice. "You guys do like I want."

He tossed the dice into the green. They rolled and slid to a halt. James blinked with surprise when he saw the face of the dice. The rest of the table groaned.

"Eleven!" a woman's voice exclaimed. "Man, you rolled a natural. I've been trying all night to do that."

James turned to face the speaker. He was glad he did. She was a lovely young black woman with skin the color of coffee blended with rich cream. Her curly black hair formed a halo around an oval face, highlighted by a wide, full mouth and big soft brown eyes.

"Then let's say I did it in your honor," James said, grinning. "Don't get jealous. It didn't do me any good."

"It would have if you hadn't tried that crazy hardway bet," she remarked, pouting. "You either like to lose or you're letting machismo get in the way of your good sense."

"What are you getting excited about?" James said, remembering the role he was trying to play. "I'm the one who lost, honey. And I'm gonna get my money back. You'll see. This table is gonna pay for my hotel room, my trip back to Detroit and a new Caddy when I get there."

"You tell 'em, brother," a baritone voice chuckled. " 'Keep the faith, baby' as Adam Clayton Powell used to say."

James glanced up at the man who spoke. The Phoenix pro needed all his willpower to conceal his astonishment when he found himself face to face with the Black Angel.

Percy Haldren was big, about six and a half feet tall and built like a black refrigerator. His face was wide with thick features and pale sand-colored eyes. A gold ring dangled from the Angel's earlobe and the infamous Damballah snake medallion hung from his bull neck. Haldren wore a bright red dinner jacket and a frilled yellow shirt. The fabric was strained by coils of muscle beneath the cloth.

"Congressman Powell spent a great deal of time on Bimini Island, you know," the Angel remarked. "As long as you're visiting the Bahamas, you should take a trip there and see the End of the World."

"Oh, yeah?" James replied. "And when is the world due to end? Like to know so I can go wacko with my credit cards."

"I mean the End of the World bar in Alice Town," Haldren replied, smiling. "Marvelous place. Perhaps I...."

The Angel's rattlesnake eyes suddenly shifted to

follow a sudden movement. The pretty lady gambler had abruptly left the table. She had a terrific body, long and lean with firm breasts emphasized by a low-cut gown. A slit up to her thigh displayed plenty of well-shaped leg. But the hardness in Haldren's expression suggested he was not impressed by her figure.

"Perhaps we can talk later," the Angel said in a mechanical voice. "Better luck with the game, Mr. . . . ?"

"Scott," James replied, giving his cover name. "Robert Scott. And you're. . . ?"

"We'll talk later, Mr. Scott," Haldren assured him. "Excuse me."

The Black Angel hurried from the table. He did not head toward the woman, but James was sure she was the reason Haldren decided to rush off. The Phoenix Force badass considered his options and made a snap decision of his own. James left the crap table and jogged after the woman.

He almost bumped into Rafael Encizo. The Cuban had been watching and had come to the same conclusion as Calvin James. Encizo was heading after the Black Angel so they could cover both bases. James was confident in the teamwork of Phoenix Force. He did not have to ask if Encizo had told Steward to get McCarter for backup.

James hurried to the corridor where the woman had vanished from view. He found a row of doors. A sour-faced swarthy man with a bandido mustache stood by one of them, arms folded on his chest.

"Hey," James began as he approached the man. "Did you see a woman run through here?"

"I ain't seen nothin', man," the man replied. He spoke with a South American accent, but James could not put a label on it.

"You didn't?" James mused. "What's behind the door?"

"None of your business, nigger," the man sneered as he slipped a hand inside his jacket. "Get the fuck outta here, boy. *Comprende?*"

"Didn't your mama teach you any manners?" James inquired. "Was she too busy servicing gringo sailors for two pesos a throw?"

The Latin snarled something under his breath as he pulled a .32 snub revolver from shoulder leather. Before he could aim the weapon, Calvin James was all over him. The black man's hands flashed, chopping the hard edges across the thug's forearm to jar the gun from the man's hands.

James snap-kicked his opponent between the legs. The Latin gasped as he doubled up and clawed at his mashed genitals. James hooked his left fist into the side of the goon's jaw and drove a right uppercut to the man's solar plexus. Then he rammed a knee into the guy's gut. The gunman started to crumple to the floor. James slashed a karate chop to his nape to make certain he did not get up for a while.

The black tornado yanked open the door. It was an exit that led to a parking lot at the rear of the casino. James unbuttoned his jacket in case he needed the Colt Commander in a hurry. He moved into the lot cautiously, wishing he had not chosen to wear a white dinner jacket. Sure as hell would reduce his ability to blend with the shadows outside.

James heard voices near the center of the lot. He shuffled to the cover of a parked sedan and crouched low as he crept along its length to get in position at the end of the vehicle where he could peer around the edge.

He saw Percy Haldren and the young black woman from the casino.

The Black Angel had twisted one of the woman's arms behind her back. He easily hauled her across the lot, roughly escorting her to a dark blue van that was parked about a hundred yards from James's position. Two men emerged from the van, and Haldren pushed her toward the pair. The Angel shoved the woman, pitching her into the two strangers. Each man grabbed one of her arms and held her.

"You two were supposed to be here twenty minutes ago," Haldren complained.

"Engine trouble," a shaggy blond man with an unkempt beard replied.

"We got here as fast as we could," his partner, a tall, wiry man with dark brown hair and a hawkbill nose, added.

"No matter," Haldren sighed. "Little Cornelia didn't get away. She didn't pay me the money she owes me, either. So now you two will have to take care of her."

"Please, Angel," the woman began. "I'll get your money, just—"

Haldren snapped an arm up sharply, striking the back of his hand across Cornelia's face. James ground his teeth together in anger when he heard the loud clap of flesh against flesh. The woman's head recoiled from the blow.

"Your time has run out, my dear," Angel sighed. "You've failed to raise the money so now you'll have to earn it."

"You're gonna learn a new profession, lady," the hawk-nosed man said as he snapped a set of handcuffs around the woman's wrists.

"And we'll start breakin' you in tonight, sweetheart," the blonde added.

"No," Cornelia gasped. "Help! Somebody hel—"

Haldren drove a short, hard punch to her slender belly. The woman gasped in breathless pain. The two henchmen quickly opened the rear doors of the van, then gathered up Cornelia and dumped her inside. The blond goon smiled as he slid a hand up Cornelia's leg.

"Nice stuff," he commented, moving his fingers to her inner thigh. "This is gonna be fun."

"Not here," Haldren snapped. "And don't get carried away. A dead woman doesn't make a very good hooker."

"We'll be careful," Hawk Nose promised.

"All right," the Angel said gruffly. "Get out of here."

"Help!" Cornelia screamed from inside the van.

"Shit," the blond thug growled as he hopped in with her. "Shut up, bitch!"

She tried to kick him in the groin, but the attack was obvious and expected. The hoodlum shifted a leg to guard his crotch, and her foot struck his thigh. His left hand snaked out to seize Cornelia's hair as he swung a right cross to her face. Knuckles met jawbone hard. Blondie raised his fist to hit her again, but her unconscious body had already sagged to the floor.

"Stay in there and keep her quiet," Hawk Nose said. "I'll drive."

The thug closed the back of the van. Haldren headed back to the casino. Calvin James had watched the incident from his hiding place. He wanted to help Cornelia, but if he rushed forward with gun in hand the hoods would have used the woman for a shield and drawn their own weapons. Putting Cornelia in the middle of a gun battle would not reduce the risk to her life.

Besides, the mission had to come first. So far James had learned that the Black Angel was a ruthless loan shark, but that did not prove Haldren was connected with the murders of Landers or Franklin. They needed the Angel alive and a sudden gun battle might force them to kill him.

But James did not intend to let the bastards kidnap the woman. He drew his Colt pistol and darted to the cover of a white Lincoln parked closer to the van.

Suddenly a projectile struck the window of the Lincoln inches from James's head. The bullet cracked a crude spiderweb pattern in the glass as the sharp *crack* of a small-caliber weapon sang out.

The unexpected attack startled Calvin James, but he was too experienced to freeze with fear. The black commando's reflexes took over. He pivoted sharply, pistol arm extended, eyes fixed on the sights of the weapon. He found his assailant—the Latin thug he had encountered in the corridor. The gunman had recovered consciousness, retrieved his .32 revolver and come looking for Calvin James—mad as hell and hungry for blood.

The Latin pointed his gun at the Phoenix fighter and prepared to pull the trigger. Years of combat-pistol training and experience under fire gave James the edge. He snap-aimed and triggered his Colt Commander. The big pistol roared. Flame burst from the muzzle. A 185-grain hollowpoint projectile smashed into the Latin's chest before he could fire his weapon.

The bullet struck sternal bone and blasted it to bits. Shrapnel exploded into the Latin killer's heart and lungs. The impact of the big .45-caliber slug lifted the man off his feet and pitched him backward into the wall of the Neptune's Palace casino.

The shots alerted Haldren and his men. The Black Angel dashed behind a red Mercedes-Benz and hastily drew a 9mm Largo pistol. The hawk-nosed henchman rushed to the front of the van, eager to get away from the gun battle.

He ran right into Rafael Encizo.

The Cuban had tailed Haldren from the casino. He had also witnessed the incident with Cornelia and waited to advance in order to rescue the woman. Encizo had already reached the front of the van when the shooting erupted. When Hawk Nose bolted for the cab, Encizo was ready for him.

The thug cursed with surprise and fear as he reached for a weapon under his Windbreaker. Encizo closed in fast and hammered the butt of his Walther PPK into the man's forearm before he could draw his gun. The Cuban's other hand shot out to drive the point of his Gerber Mark I under the hoodlum's jaw. The blade pierced the hollow of the man's throat.

Percy Haldren caught a glimpse of Calvin James's white dinner jacket. He immediately aimed his Largo autoloader and triggered two rapid-fire rounds at the black warrior. The Black Angel was not much of a marksman. One 9mm slug shattered the rear window of the Lincoln James was using for cover. The other bullet struck the trunk, pierced the metal skin and buried itself in a spare tire inside.

Rafael Encizo did not have a clear target, but he snapped off two quick shots at Haldren to get the evil angel's attention away from James. A .380 projectile ricocheted off the steel skin of the red Mercedes and hissed past Haldren's face. The Black Angel's hands trembled as he returned fire. His shot went high, traveling somewhere into the velvet night above.

Calvin James aimed his Colt Commander and opened fire. A big .45 slug smashed a side window of the Mercedes. Haldren could barely see from the cold sweat that dripped into his eyes as he triggered two panicked shots in the general direction of James's position.

The back door of the van burst open. The blond thug used the door for a shield as he poked the barrel of a .357 Magnum around the edge and fired at Encizo's position. The 137-grain slug missed the Cuban by almost a foot, sparking against concrete on impact.

Blondie fired another Magnum round at James. The high-velocity bullet broke the glass in the front window of the Lincoln and burrowed through the upholstery on the car door.

"Oh, shit!" James exclaimed when the .357 missile popped an exit hole less than an inch below his right elbow. "I hate it when that happens."

The tawny-haired killer knew he would not hit either of the mysterious gunmen hidden among the cars in the lot, but he hoped to pin them down long enough for reinforcements to arrive. He forgot about Cornelia. Only personal survival mattered now.

Cornelia moaned softly as she regained consciousness. Her face and lower abdomen ached. Tears crept from the corners of her eyes, but she did not sob aloud. The sound of gunshots warned her of danger even before the cobwebs in her mind fell aside to allow her to recall what had happened before she was knocked senseless.

She opened her eyes and found herself on the floor of the van. Her hands were cuffed behind her back. The front of her gown had been ripped open to expose her ripe breasts and her dress was bunched up to her waist. She glanced toward the entrance and saw one of her tormentors poised at the threshold.

The honky bastard had his back turned to her and he appeared to be shooting at somebody. He did not want to expose himself to the open, so she guessed somebody outside might take a shot at him if they got a decent target. Cornelia slowly rose to her feet, fearful the pounding of her heart would betray her.

She acted quickly, afraid that she would freeze up if she waited. Cornelia ran two steps and slammed a stocking-clad foot into the small of the thug's back. The kick sent him hurtling out of the van. The creep hit the ground hard and rolled away from the vehicle.

Calvin James instantly took advantage of this opportunity. He aimed his pistol and pumped two .45 slugs into the bastard. One slug struck the guy's right shoulder, tearing through deltoid muscle to smash the bones beneath. The other bullet crashed into his upper lip, shattering the philtrum and driving jawbone splinters up into his brain. The hoodlum thrashed about like a decapitated snake before death brought his body to full halt.

The Black Angel had had enough. He bolted to the casino and yanked a door open. Encizo fired a hasty shot at the fleeing loan shark. The .380 round whined against the doorway as Haldren ducked inside the building.

"Son of a bitch got away," James growled as he jogged toward the van. "Everybody okay?"

"I'm pissed off that I missed Haldren," Encizo replied as he inserted a fresh magazine into the butt of his PPK. "But otherwise I'm all right."

James moved to the rear of the van and gazed up at the shivering figure of Cornelia. Her lovely face was bruised and some blood had trickled from the corner of her mouth, but she did not appear to be injured.

"You," Cornelia said thickly, staring back at James. "You're the dude who can't roll dice worth a damn. What are you, a cop?"

"A friend," he replied with a smile. "Just relax. Nobody is going to hurt you anymore. . . ."

The sound of full-auto weapons inside the Neptune's Palace casino abruptly drew James's attention to the building.

"What the hell is going on in there?" he muttered.

"I don't know," Encizo replied. "But I bet I can guess who's right in the middle of it."

"Yeah," James said with a nod, aware that McCarter was still inside the casino. "Let's go see if he needs a hand."

6

David McCarter had never won so much money at a baccarat table before. He kept getting eights and nines, and his bank kept getting larger and larger. The Briton was disgusted. He had to lose and lose big or the night would be a total waste.

Then Lieutenant Steward appeared by McCarter's chair to tell him an emergency had come up. The Briton immediately excused himself and passed the shoe.

"What about your chips?" a player inquired.

"And what about giving us a chance to break even?" another added.

"You blokes take the bloody chips and do what you want with them," McCarter replied as he left the table. "Hasn't done me any good, anyway. All I've been able to do is win all night."

"What did he say?" the German card player asked the others at the table.

"Pay it no heed," a Frenchman said with a shrug. "The English are all a bit mad, *non*?"

McCarter and Steward prepared to follow Encizo and James to provide assistance if needed. However, a large man dressed in a shabby suit blocked their path before they could cross the casino floor.

"You two seem in a hurry," the man remarked. The accent was from somewhere in the United States, but

McCarter could not pinpoint it because the guy sounded as if he had a throatful of gravel. "What's the rush?"

"Urgent business," McCarter confirmed. "Where's the loo?"

"That's the bathroom, ain't it?" the goon asked with a grin. "You gotta have a conference to decide when you'll go to the bathroom? You just like to hold each other's dick or somethin'?"

"Don't get nasty," McCarter warned. "Or I'll hit you with my purse."

"Cute," the big man grunted. "You guys done a lot of cute stuff since you come in here with the nigger and the spic. We been watchin' you clowns. Figure you're up to somethin'."

"And you're the Minister for Moral Conduct?" the Briton inquired with a grin.

"I work for the casino, asshole," the big man stated. "Sometimes I bust heads, so don't fuck with me. The boss wants to talk to you, and you'd better have the right answers."

Two more large men stepped up behind the gorilla with the raspy voice. One of them opened his jacket to reveal the grip of a revolver thrust in his belt. McCarter was not sure how to handle the situation. He did not want a public scene, but he could not abandon his partners in a time of need, either.

"Perhaps we could step outside and talk about settling this matter," the Briton suggested.

"Cocky bastard, ain't he, Sal?" one of the underlings snorted. "Little shit wants to duke it out with us."

"I was thinking of a financial arrangement," McCarter explained.

"We ain't interested," Sal spoke for his men. "You

can try to bribe the boss, but it won't get you nowhere neither. Now come on!''

Then the gunfight outside the casino began. The sound of several different pistols snarling from the parking lot startled everyone inside the Neptune's Palace. Shouts of alarm filled the casino as customers jumped from seats. The three muscle boys turned their heads toward the shots.

McCarter quickly took advantage of the distraction. His right hand became a blur as he suddenly drew the Browning Hi-Power from the Bianchi rig under his left arm. The Briton stepped forward and swung a backhand sweep, swatting the steel barrel across Sal's jaw.

The unexpected blow staggered the big thug. McCarter did not give him time to recover. The Briton's hand shoved Sal off balance, pushing him into one of the other hoods. At the same instant, McCarter pointed the Browning at the third man's face and thumbed off the safety catch.

The guy was dumb, but he had guts. He pulled the revolver from his belt. McCarter triggered the Browning and drilled a 9mm parabellum round through the thug's forehead. The bullet punched through the gunman's skull as if it was made of papier mâché. The revolver tumbled from lifeless fingers, and its owner dropped to the floor dead.

''Jesus,'' Steward gasped, stunned by McCarter's actions.

Sal and the other goon reached for their pistols. The underling was faster than his commander and cleared leather first. McCarter's Browning snarled before the goon could aim his piece. A parabellum slug smashed into the man's throat, crushing the Adam's apple and bursting vertebrae at the base of his neck.

"Sweet Mother!" Sal whispered in awe. He raised his empty hands in surrender. "I quit, fella. You win."

Suddenly a door opened and a man armed with a Heckler & Koch machine pistol charged into the casino. Another thug stationed himself at the doorway, holding a 1911A1 Colt pistol in a two-hand Weaver's grip. The machine gunner aimed his weapon at McCarter.

The Briton saw the movement out of the corner of an eye. He whirled, swinging the Browning at the killer. Even as he moved, McCarter knew he was too late. He folded a leg and collapsed to the floor as the thug triggered his H&K blaster.

A volley of 9mm hailstones sizzled above McCarter's prone form. Bullets splintered the corner of the baccarat table. The French card player cried out in agony as two parabellum slugs slammed into his upper torso. The man fell against the table, scattering multicolored chips in all directions.

McCarter fired the Browning twice, pumping two 9mm slugs into the machine gunner's solar plexus. The 115-grain devastators burrowed upward into the chest cavity to burst the thug's heart. His body recoiled against the open door, slid across the panels and slumped lifeless to the crimson carpet.

The flunky with the Colt autoloader had instinctively jumped back into the next room. Angry and frightened, he hastily extended his gun arm and snapped a quick shot in McCarter's general direction. A .45 slug struck the frame of a chair—which, fortunately, was no longer occupied.

Lieutenant Steward had unsheathed a Walther PP automatic from its shoulder holster. The SIS officer aimed the compact pistol and squeezed off three shots as quickly as he could. Steward was not fast, and he lacked McCarter's experience and combat skill. But he was accurate. All three 7.65mm rounds struck the hoodlum in the chest, left of center. The thug fired his big Colt as he fell back into the room. The 1911A1 bellowed fiercely, blasting a harmless bullet into the ceiling.

"I don't see any more of the bastards," Steward declared, watching dozens of gamblers bolt for the exits.

"Get down, damn it!" McCarter snapped as he slithered under a blackjack table.

Sal had also hit the deck when he saw the machine gunner charge into the melee, well aware that full-auto bullets tend to be indiscriminate killers. He'd taken advantage of the time McCarter had been preoccupied trading lead with the gunman and crawled to the cover of a craps table where he finally drew a .38 Colt snub nose.

The heavyweight hood cautiously peered around the edge of a table leg. Christ, the shit had really hit the fan, he thought. Sal did not want to tangle with the Limey. That guy was quicker than a cobra and armed with a big 9mm pistol. A lot of those guns have a capacity for fourteen or fifteen rounds before you had to reload. Sal was not sure how many shots McCarter had fired, but it was sure as hell fewer than that.

Suddenly Percy Haldren dashed through the corridor and stumbled into the casino. The Black Angel was running scared, in search of a safe port. Instead, he found the Neptune's Palace shot up and several corpses already littering the floor.

"Drop your gun!" Steward commanded, pointing his pistol at Haldren. "SIS. You're under arrest!"

The Black Angel let his Largo autoloader fall to the

carpet. He slowly raised his arms in surrender. Steward took a step forward. Sal aimed his diminutive revolver with care and squeezed the trigger.

"Get down!" McCarter shouted instructions once more.

The sound of his voice was lost amid the report of Sal's .38. Steward cried out when the 125-grain flat-nosed missile punched into his midsection. The SIS man doubled up and fell to one knee, wrapping his left arm around his wounded torso.

McCarter automatically pointed his Browning at the muzzle-flash of Sal's revolver. He shifted to the right and the front sight of his High-Power found Sal's grinning face. McCarter fired twice. Sal's head exploded, splattering blood and brains across the nearest wall.

A mirror shattered, the glass flew outward to the tune of an automatic rifle. The thug behind the mirror had abruptly shot it out with an M-16 assault rifle. He used the barrel to knock some jagged remnants from the frame as he knelt to use it for a bench rest.

The hood opened fire and full-auto 5.56mm rounds filled the casino. The guy acted as if he had never heard of 3-round bursts. He simply sprayed the place with bullets. McCarter stayed low and ducked his head as slugs chewed at the blackjack table above him.

Several rounds hit Lieutenant Steward. Blood poured from his bullet-torn chest as the impact of multiple slugs kicked his body across the casino floor. McCarter cursed under his breath. If the SIS officer had still been alive, he sure as hell wasn't now.

The Briton felt vibrations ride along the floor beneath the carpet. He peered between the forest of table and chair legs. Polished black shoes and pant cuffs advanced. More thugs on the Neptune's Palace payroll. McCarter wondered who was really pulling the strings, but at the moment it didn't really matter. They were trying to kill him and that was all he had to know.

"There's another one hidin' out among the tables!" the man with the M-16 shouted. "Watch yourselves. I don't think I got him yet."

"Flush 'im out," a scar-faced thug with a sawed-off pump shotgun replied. "We'll get the bastard!"

"Right!" the rifleman confirmed.

The bellow of a large-caliber handgun exploded from the opposite end of the casino. The button man with the M-16 screamed when a .45 slug ripped into his chest. The heavy 185-grain torpedo smashed through a rib and nosedived into the guy's lungs. He dropped the M-16 and clasped both hands to his chest. Pink froth bubbled from his lips as he sunk below the frame of the shattered mirror.

"Oh, fuck!" the shotgunner exclaimed as he glimpsed Calvin James's white dinner jacket moving behind the roulette table.

He immediately pointed the sawed-off Winchester pump and pulled the trigger. The shotgun boomed like the voice of doom. Buckshot tore the roulette wheel apart, sending a shower of black plastic chips and chrome shards flying from the table. The shooter rapidly worked the pump to eject a spent shell casing and insert another round of double O buck in the chamber.

"When I make that sum-bitch hop," the shotgun man told three pistol-packing henchmen, "you be ready to burn the bastard."

He extended the Winchester and prepared to pull the trigger just as a pistol popped from a different position.

Two .380 missiles pierced the shotgunner's right arm. One tore through biceps muscle while the other drilled into the guy's elbow, shattering the bony joint. The hoodlum screamed as the shotgun tumbled from his grasp. He stumbled back against a wall, clutching his wrecked arm.

Rafael Encizo was pleased with his marksmanship. He had fired his Walther PPK, hoping to wound and disable rather than kill. Phoenix Force needed answers to questions and a corpse cannot be interrogated.

One of the surviving gunmen aimed a .357 Magnum at the muzzle-flash of Encizo's pistol and squeezed off a shot. But the Cuban had already moved to the cover of a pillar and the hood's bullet sought its mark in vain. The .357 round finally connected with a mirror, blasting the glass to bits.

McCarter thrust his Browning out from under the blackjack table and triggered the weapon twice. Two parabellums struck the man with the Magnum. The thug's lower jaw burst into a shower of bones, teeth and blood. The buttonman's .357 flew from open hands as he fell to the floor.

The two remaining gunmen decided the only way to survive was to retreat. They bolted across the lobby toward the front door. Encizo charged after the pair. He thrust the Walther in his belt and ducked to scoop up the Heckler & Koch machine pistol discarded by a slain assailant. The Cuban raised the H&K blaster as he ran and fired a quick volley.

Nine-millimeter slugs pelted the ceiling and snapped at the cables supporting a chandelier. The light fixture broke free and plunged to the floor in front of the two fleeing hoodlums. Glass exploded on impact, sending flying slivers up at the enemy gunmen.

"My eyes!" one man cried, throwing down his pistol to clasp both hands to his bloodied face. "Oh, my God! I'm blind!"

The other thug whirled and swung his .38 Ruger revolver toward the casino. But James was waiting for him and fired his Commander. A .45 round slammed into the hood's thigh just above the knee. The man shrieked and tumbled to the floor, his gun slipping from trembling fingers. McCarter rushed forward and kicked it beyond the guy's reach before he could make a grab for it.

"Shit," James exclaimed. "I think Haldren got away."

"We'd better follow his example before the police arrive," Encizo suggested. "Let's take the wounded still able to talk and get the hell out of here."

"Be a little crowded in the Mercedes," McCarter commented. "Make a mess of the upholstery, too."

"No problem," James told him. "The enemy was considerate enough to leave us a nice nondescript van large enough to use as a paddy wagon."

"Then let's be on our way," the Briton agreed with a wry grin. "But you have to admit the nightlife in Nassau is terribly exciting."

7

"I thought you people would be subtle, damn it!" Maj. Pendexter Alby exclaimed. "The police report claims there were almost a dozen bodies discovered at the Neptune's Palace. Do you call that subtle?"

"It was necessary, Major," Yakov Katzenelenbogen replied simply, lighting a cigarette. "My men were forced to defend themselves. They had no choice."

"And I must defend the Bahamas," Alby snapped. "I will not allow your team to turn Nassau into a slaughterhouse."

"Would you rather allow terrorists to get away with murder?" Gary Manning inquired as he helped himself to a cup of coffee.

"Terrorists!" Alby exclaimed as he rolled his eyes with frustration. "Your three chums got in a gun battle with a bunch of gangsters, not terrorists."

"Sometimes a gangster can be a terrorist, as well," Katz commented, thoughtfully clicking the hooks of his prosthesis together. "Not surprising when one considers the fact that both are criminals."

"You're groping for justification," Alby declared. "Terrorists are anarchists and fanatics."

"Fanatics, yes," Yakov agreed. "But very few terrorists consider themselves to be anarchists. Most are political or religious extremists. However, during the

Red Brigade trials in Italy in the late 1970s, various Mafia members and former mafiosi were discovered to be connected with the terrorists.''

"There's no proof the BACO terrorists exist!" the major insisted. "Tonight's gun battle proves nothing."

"It proved that the Neptune's Palace casino was crawling with gunmen armed with some pretty fancy hardware," Manning stated. "Or do you still think the CIA are the only bad guys in town?"

"The Black Angel is a loan shark and probably involved in cocaine traffic," Alby conceded gruffly. "We knew that before your people pushed him. All you've accomplished is a senseless slaughter. And Lieutenant Steward is among the dead, goddammit."

"I'm sorry about your man, Major," Katz assured him. "But none of us knew the personnel at the casino were dangerous. You must admit that our men stumbled onto something bigger than a local loan-shark operation."

"Perhaps," Alby allowed. "But I doubt that it will be worth the price already paid in human blood."

"I'm very familiar with that price," the Israeli said grimly. "Believe it or not, there are things worth it. Now, let's see if the others are ready."

The three men left the tiny, poorly furnished office of the warehouse. Phoenix Force had insisted on a safe-house outside the city limits of Nassau. The warehouse was the best the Bahamian Security Intelligence Service could come up with on short notice. For their part, the men of Phoenix Force were more than satisfied with the place.

The warehouse was a rental from the New Providence National Freight Unlimited Corporation, which rented dozens of storage buildings every year. Most of their customers were American or European businessmen, so no one would be suspicious or even particularly interested in what the place was being used for.

It was remote enough to keep activities from the eyes and ears of the curious. The warehouse had a large bay area and several smaller rooms that conveniently lacked windows. It also had electricity and indoor plumbing.

Katz, Manning and Alby met David McCarter in the bay area. The Briton had changed clothes, happy to be rid of the stuffy tuxedo. He was far more comfortable dressed in a bush shirt and khaki trousers. McCarter didn't like being unarmed: the Browning was sheathed in a brown leather holster on his right hip.

"Where's everybody else gotten to, Mr. Daniels?" Katz inquired.

"Mr. Scott patched up our guests well enough for us to interrogate them," McCarter answered, replying to his cover name and using Calvin James's alias as he spoke. "Then he drove back to the little coffeehouse on Nassau Avenue where we dropped off the girl. I think he's planning to take her home. Probably won't see him until some time after daybreak."

"Who's going to administer the scopolamine?" Manning asked.

"Scopolamine?" Alby said with a frown. "That's a pretty powerful drug. I understand it can be fatal if mishandled."

"It is risky," Katz confirmed. "But scopolamine is the only reliable truth serum. Mr. Scott is a trained medical man, and he's the only person on my team qualified to use the drug in an emergency."

"Scott doesn't think we should use the scopolamine

on the prisoners," McCarter explained. "All three of them are wounded, you know. Had to treat one of them for shock."

"Wasn't one of them blinded?" Alby inquired, a trace of disgust creeping into his voice. "Was it necessary to poke a man's eye out, Mr. Daniels?"

"Happened by accident," the Briton replied with a shrug. "And the bloke isn't blind. He was hit in the face by some flying glass. One piece got in the corner of his right eye and the chap panicked, convinced he'd been blinded. Scott gave him some morphine and took the splinter out. Then he washed the fella's eyes and bandaged them. Scott is sure the bloke's eyes will be fine, but he doesn't think we should use scopolamine on the chap because his heart probably wouldn't take the additional strain."

"We can't use it, anyway, since Scott left," Manning commented. "So how are we going to interrogate these clowns?"

"Oh, Mr. Rodriguez and I have a plan for that," McCarter said with a grin. "In fact, we found something at the casino to help us. Stuffed it in the trunk of the Mercedes and brought it with us just for this purpose."

"I'm not going to stand by and let you torture these prisoners," Alby declared sharply.

"Who said anything about torture?" the Briton replied, clearly annoyed. "We're fighting men, not sadists. Torture isn't our style, mate."

"Are any of the prisoners fit enough to interrogate?" Katz inquired.

"The one with the leg wound," McCarter replied. "We put him in a quiet little room all by himself in order to let him sweat for a while."

"Guy might pass out before he can talk," Manning said.

"Not a chance," the Briton assured him. "Scott gave him enough Benzedrine to make sure of that. So let's figure out how we want to play this scene and see if he'll break."

THE HOOD'S NAME was Vince Natwick, a white Bahamian low-life. He was seated in an armchair, wrists cuffed to the armrests and upper torso bound to the back. A naked 100-watt light bulb burned down on the sweaty thug. His head jerked about sharply when the door opened.

"Hello," Colonel Katzenelenbogen greeted, waving with the steel hook of his prosthesis. "Thought you might be getting lonely in here by yourself."

"I want my lawyer," Natwick replied hoarsely. "And I want a doctor, too. If you don't get me to a hospital, I'll sue you bastards. . . ."

"You can't sue us because you don't know who we are," Gary Manning said dryly. "Your driver's license says you're Vincent R. Natwick. Is that your real name?"

"Piss off," the thug snapped.

"That's no way to talk to the fellows who want to help you," Katz commented.

"You can help me by getting me a lawyer," Natwick insisted. "I know my bleedin' rights, you one-armed sod."

"Look," Manning began. "You're going to spend some time in jail. Cooperate and you'll only have to spend a year or two in protective custody. We can arrange for you to serve time in the United States so you won't have to worry about getting a knife in the ribs for ratting on your pals."

"I'm not telling you bastards a goddamn thing," the hood insisted.

"Are you afraid?" Katz asked. "If so, you're scared of the wrong people. Right now, you have more to fear from us than you do from your fellow criminals."

"Don't threaten me," Natwick scoffed. "This is the Bahamas, not Nazi Germany or a fuckin' Turkish prison. You blokes might beat the hell out of me, but you won't do anything too drastic."

"Why not?" the Israeli said with a shrug. "Haven't you figured out that we're not with the police? Savages like you don't play by the rules, and neither do we."

"You got me trembling in me boots," the thug sneered.

A scream suddenly echoed from the bay area outside. Natwick stiffened, eyes wide with alarm. Even Katz and Manning were startled by the blood-chilling shriek, although they knew what it was.

"What. . . ." Natwick began, but he clamped his mouth shut before he could finish the sentence.

"I guess one of your friends is also being stubborn," Manning sighed. "Daniels and Rodriguez aren't as patient as we are."

McCarter appeared at the doorway. "No need for alarm, mates," the Briton assured them. "Ramon and I are fine. Bloke we were questioning just got a bit out of hand. Son of a bitch still wouldn't talk so Ramon cut his throat."

"Damn it, Daniels!" Katz snapped. "I told you two we wanted to keep these characters alive. No one is to be executed unless I order it."

"Don't get high and mighty with me," the Briton growled. "I remember what you did in El Salvador when you lost your temper."

"I'm not gonna fall for this bullshit," Natwick declared, his voice trembling slightly. "This is all an act."

"Really?" Katz smiled thinly. "Then maybe we should show you a little proof to convince you we're not playing games. Daniels, you and Rodriguez fetch the fellow you killed. Bring him here to meet Mr. Natwick."

"But he's a bloody mess..." McCarter complained.

"I don't care if his guts are hanging out," the Israeli snapped. "Do it!"

McCarter left the room. A few minutes later he returned with Rafael Encizo. The two men dragged a lifeless figure across the threshold. They dumped the corpse on the floor. The dead man's throat and shirt were splashed with crimson. Sightless eyes stared up at Natwick.

"My God," the hoodlum gasped, gazing at the deep cut in the throat of the corpse. "It's Jacobson! You bastards murdered him in cold blood!"

"He tried to get tough," Encizo stated with a cruel smile. "But he wasn't so tough after all."

"Is this chap trying to be tough, too?" McCarter asked, tilting his head toward Natwick.

"So far," Katz answered, "but we've just—"

"For crissake!" Natwick exclaimed, still staring at the corpse. "I'll talk! I'll tell you everything I know, but you have to promise you'll protect me from them."

"You've got our word on that," Manning assured him.

"Not just sending me to the States," Natwick declared. "They'll get me there. If I have to stand trial, they'll know and they'll get me anywhere I might run. The United States, Europe, South America. It won't make any difference. They're everywhere."

"Who are they?" Katz asked.

"MERGE," the hoodlum replied. "They call themselves MERGE. I don't know much about it except it's *big*. Very big."

"What do you know?" the Canadian demanded.

"MERGE has organized all the small, independent syndicates in the Bahamas," Natwick answered. "The Neptune's Palace was a front for loan sharking and cocaine peddling. The casino attracted the right crowd to make it profitable."

"Where do we find the leaders of MERGE?" Katz asked.

"I don't know," Natwick said. "Hell, I was just a minor-league soldier. The Black Angel could tell you more. He was my boss and he was just a flunky working for MERGE. It's a huge organization, bigger than the Mafia before that crazy Vietnam veteran busted it up. You know, the bloke they called the Executioner?"

"We've heard of him," Encizo said dryly.

"As a matter of fact," Natwick continued, "quite a few of the chaps I met at the casino were Yanks. They never said they were Mafia, but the rest of us always figured they were former mob soldiers. The Colombian Syndicate is involved, too. That's where the coke comes from. But the syndicate is just part of MERGE."

"Do you know anything about the assassination of Congressman Franklin or a man named Fred Landers?" Manning inquired.

"I heard about Franklin," the hood said. "They say he was killed by terrorists, but I reckon MERGE could have done it. Landers's name sounds familiar. Was he that bloke from the American Embassy what got blown up in his car?"

"That's right," Encizo confirmed.

"Landers was a regular customer of the Black Angel," Natwick stated. "Gambled a lot. Real fond of nose candy, too. The Angel didn't kill Landers, but he could probably tell you who had it done."

"Where can we find somebody who knows more about this MERGE outfit?" Manning asked.

"The Angel is the only contact I know about for sure," Natwick replied. "It doesn't pay to get too curious about MERGE. Something you blokes better think about if you're considering going after the organization. Believe me, you can't win. All you'll get if you tangle with MERGE is one thing—*dead*."

The four men of Phoenix Force locked Natwick in the room. Major Alby was not in the bay area so they took advantage of the opportunity to converse privately.

"What do you think, Katz?" Manning asked. "Figure this MERGE business is for real?"

"I don't think he was lying," the Israeli replied. "When David and Rafael dragged that corpse into the room it rattled Natwick's cage too badly for him to come up with such an imaginative story off the top of his pointy little head."

"I wonder what he'd say if he knew Rafael had knifed that bloke in the throat back at the casino and we brought the body here to play our little bluff," McCarter mused.

"How'd you guys manage the fresh blood on the man's throat and shirt?" Manning asked.

"We got it from Calvin's medical supply," Encizo answered. "He used quite a bit of it while he was doctoring up the wounded men, but there was still enough left over for our charade."

"Speaking of Calvin," Katz began. "I hope he gets

back soon. We'd better be at full strength. If MERGE is half as powerful as Natwick claims it is, we've just encountered the tip of a very dangerous iceberg.''

8

Calvin James rocked his pelvis, working himself deeper as the lovely lady beneath him moaned happily. Cornelia Ambrose wrapped her long shapely legs around his hips, locking her ankles at the small of James's back. Her body began to tremble and buck as her nails bit into his skin.

"Ooh, baby," she gasped. "Don't stop."

"Why would I wanta stop?" James whispered breathlessly.

He increased the tempo of his thrusts. Cornelia cried out with delight as he drove himself faster and harder into the center of her womanhood. Her body thrashed against the sheets as a wild orgasm swept through her. James climaxed seconds later, groaning with pleasure when he released his seed within Cornelia's womb. They lay on the mattress, locked in a tender embrace, breathing hard and pleasantly exhausted.

"You're really terrific, Bob," Cornelia sighed. "But I bet your name isn't really Robert Scott."

"Why do you say that?" James asked. "Isn't your name really Cornelia Ambrose?"

"I'm not running around Nassau with a gun," she replied. "What are you, Bob? Some sort of secret agent or maybe a detective?"

"Like Sam Spade?" James laughed.

"I'm serious," she insisted. "Who are you? What are

you and your friends doing in Nassau, getting into gun-fights with hoods?''

"You ask so many questions," James sighed. "But none of the important stuff like whether I'll respect you in the morning or what sign was I born under. Hell, you haven't even asked me if I snore. . . ."

"Okay," Cornelia said, shaking her head. "I suppose you're entitled to keep your secrets since you saved my life back at the Neptune's Palace. You don't want to tell me anything, then don't tell me shit, fella."

"I can't tell you about myself or why I'm here," James explained. "All I can say is I'm part of a special unit and our work is top secret. If I told you any details about what we do it might put your life in danger."

"I'm kinda used to that," Cornelia remarked. "To-night's run-in with the Black Angel wasn't the first time I've had trouble with loan sharks."

"Loan sharks are bad news," James stated. "But Per-cy Haldren is a candyass sissy compared to some of the two-legged monsters that we come up against. There are men who would murder a thousand people for a small profit. Some would do it just for fun. They thrive on fear, death and destruction."

"The forces of evil, huh?" she said as she grinned.

"You'd better believe it," he said sternly. "There real-ly are demons, but you don't have to take a trip to hell to find them. They like to crush things just so they can hear the bones crunch. They're arrogant, ignorant and vicious."

Cornelia shuddered. "Sounds like you know about some things I'd just as soon not hear about," she said. "Ignorance might not always be bliss, but I think I'll sleep better at night if I don't know about some things."

"Well, if you ever do think about those things," the Phoenix Force pro began, "it might help you sleep at night if you bear in mind that there are watchdogs to protect you from such organized evil. And we fight fire with fire."

"I got a glimpse of you guys in action," she commented. "I almost feel sorry for the other side."

"You don't need to," James replied. "They don't feel sorry for anyone. But we've talked about what I do. What about you?"

"You mean what do I do when I'm not getting in trouble with loan sharks in Nassau?" Cornelia smiled. "I'm usually getting into trouble with loan sharks back in the States."

"Sounds to me like you'd better quit gambling," James told her.

"Hey, that's my problem," she said sharply. "You've got enough of your own to worry about."

"None of my business, huh?" James asked, raising his eyebrows. "I guess it was none of my business when those dudes were using you for a punching bag, either. Maybe you don't realize that my partners and I risked our lives to help you. Those guys were shooting real bullets at us."

"Look, I'm grateful for what you did," Cornelia assured him. "It's just I don't need a sermon on the evils of gambling. I've heard it all before."

"I'm not going to give you a sermon," he told her. "And I don't think gambling is evil, but compulsive behavior can be downright destructive. Alcohol, drugs, gambling can ruin your life when you can't control them."

"So you figure I should join the Salvation Army or

Gamblers Anonymous and start singing in the church choir?''

"I think you'd better stop gambling before it gets you killed," James replied. "But that's a decision you'll have to make on your own. What do you do for a living, Cornelia?"

"I'm a sales representative for Farrel Cosmetics," she replied. "Won a trip to the Bahamas this year."

"You must be pretty good at your job," James remarked. "Do you enjoy it?"

"I don't know," Cornelia answered. "Never really thought about enjoying work. I mean, you work to make a living. It isn't supposed to be fun."

"But gambling is supposed to be fun," the commando said. "So you figure that's a way to enjoy yourself?"

"Look, Bob," she began, "I was born and raised in Los Angeles. Do you know how many black girls from my neighborhood wound up as hookers or drug addicts or both? A lot of them are dead now."

"Lady, I know all about being poor and being black," James told her. "And it doesn't mean you have to self destruct."

"You figure you're gonna live to a ripe old age by running around fighting gangsters or Russian spies or whatever you do?" Cornelia demanded. "I'll have you know I've won some big money by gambling. One day I'll win real big. Then I'll. . . ."

"Go out and gamble it all away." James sighed. "Don't you see that no matter how many times you win, in the long run you'll always lose? You should find another hobby or get a job that you really enjoy."

"You make it sound easy," she muttered. "Not every employer is eager to hire a black woman."

"I didn't say it would be easy," James told her. "Few things worthwhile are easy. Black people can get any kind of job in the world, but they don't accomplish a damn thing by giving up."

"Maybe. . . ." Cornelia began.

Suddenly, Calvin James leaped from the bed. Naked, he dashed to the pile of clothes at the foot of the bed and reached for the Colt Commander sheathed in a Jackass Leather rig. The black warrior had heard metal scrape metal. He reacted instantly, even before he realized the sound came from the door to Cornelia's apartment.

James yanked the Colt from its holster as the door swung open. Two men stood at the threshold. A small rat-faced man knelt by the doorway, a set of steel lock picks still in his hands. The other guy was big and muscular with a dark olive complexion. The thug reached under his jacket for a piece, but froze when James pointed the Commander at him.

"Try it, asshole," the black warrior invited.

"Cristo," the goon growled as he used two fingers to slowly draw a snub nose .357 from his belt.

He dropped the gun to the carpet and kicked it across the floor toward James. The muscle boy raised his hands in surrender. His rat-faced partner tossed down his burglar tools.

"Easy, fella," he urged, holding his hands high.

"Face the wall," James instructed. "Spread-eagled. You guys know the routine."

"Let's talk," the big man suggested as he stepped forward. "The Angel sent us for the girl. This doesn't concern you."

"Take one more step and you're dead, dipshit," James warned.

"What does the woman matter to you?" the thug asked. "We can pay you to let us take her. You can make a profit by cooperating, or you can make enemies. Very bad enemies."

"Just shut up and..." James began.

The rat-man suddenly pulled a small automatic from his hip pocket. The little hoodlum fumbled with the safety catch and pointed the pistol at James. The Colt Commander exploded. A .45 slug burst through the bridge of the man's rat face. The bullet burned through brain matter and smashed open the back of the creep's skull.

The larger man moved fast. He rushed James and grabbed the black man's wrist before the Phoenix fighter could track him with his pistol. The thug's left fist connected with the side of James's jaw. The hoodlum shoved James's arm toward the floor and slammed the wrist across his knee.

James's hand opened, dropping the .45 autoloader. The black warrior quickly whipped the heel of his left palm under the Latin killer's jaw. The blow staggered the big man. James delivered a left-legged hook kick to his opponent's midsection. The goon groaned. Then the black warrior pivoted sharply and thrust a powerful side kick, driving his right foot into the man's chest.

The thug stumbled backward into a small table. Snarling like a wounded bear, the man seized an adjacent chair and charged forward, raising the furniture over his head.

Calvin James shuffled toward his attacker and launched another kick. His genitals swung free, vulnerable to attack as his leg shot out in a high thrust. The bottom of his bare foot smashed into the hood's face. The kick sent the goon hurtling back into a wall.

Blood flowed freely from both nostrils as he dropped the chair.

James closed in and swung a right cross to his opponent's jaw, and the thug slid along the wall into a corner. James snapped a ball-of-the-foot kick at the hoodlum's solar plexus. The tae kwon-do stroke missed its mark and struck the man's forearm. The goon suddenly charged, swinging a clawed hand at James's testicles.

The Phoenix warrior snapped a knee up to protect his manhood. He felt sharp pain as the hoodlum's nails raked skin. James whipped a bent elbow under the thug's jawbone. The man's head snapped back from the blow, exposing his throat.

James's hand slashed like a sword. The hard edge caught the hoodlum across the windpipe, caving in the thyroid cartilage. The Latin killer gasped, blood bubbling from his gaping mouth. He clasped both hands to his crushed throat as he wilted to the carpet.

Suddenly two uniformed figures burst into the room. Service revolvers drawn and held ready. The wide-eyed cops aimed their weapons at the naked black man who stood in the center of the room. James knew better than to startle a pair of nervous policemen with guns in their hands. He raised his hands and nodded at the officers.

"Don't move," one of the cops warned.

"I really can explain this," James told them.

"Turn around and face the wall," the other cop ordered.

"What are you gonna do?" Calvin James sighed as he followed instructions. "Search me?"

9

The sun climbed higher in the blue Bahamian sky as David McCarter drove the black Mercedes from the Nassau police station. The Briton and Colonel Yakov Katzenelenbogen had arrived an hour earlier to get Calvin James out of jail. The cops had checked with Major Alby at SIS headquarters and reluctantly released the black commando and even returned his .45 Colt and shoulder holster.

"Man, I hate jail cells," James commented. "I hate making an ass of myself, too. Sorry you guys had to come get me."

"No problem," Katz assured him. "But you'd better not see that woman again. If she doesn't get you in trouble, you're apt to attract some to her."

"I know," James sighed with regret. "Cornelia is heading back to the States, anyway. I had a talk with her at the cop station, and she agreed it was best to go back home. She's got some personal problems that need to be taken care of, but at least she's able to admit that now. I'd like to see her again after she beats her compulsion to gamble. She's really a hell of a lady."

"Maybe you'll get a chance to see her after we finish this mission," Katz replied. "But I'm afraid this chicken-shit little assignment might turn out to be a lot bigger than we imagined."

"Oh?" James raised his eyebrows. "What happened?"

The Israeli explained about Natwick's confession and the thumbnail sketch of the sinister crime network that called itself MERGE.

"Jesus," the black man muttered. "Are you convinced this business is true? This MERGE outfit really exists?"

"I think so," Katz confirmed. "And it's not really surprising that an organization like MERGE has been created. Mack Bolan crushed the Mafia several years ago, but individual mafioso have been popping up in terrorist groups and small syndicates ever since. Everybody thinks the Executioner is dead, and Bolan hasn't been much of a threat to organized crime for the last year or so. He's too busy just trying to stay alive. The remnants of the Mafia have had ample time to rebuild their shadow empire."

"But Bolan killed off hundreds of mobsters," James said, familiar with the Executioner's career. "Where did the Mafia get enough experienced manpower and connections to become an international network again?"

"The answer to that is found in the very name MERGE," the Israeli explained. "The remnants of the Mafia families have conducted a merger with other criminal syndicates. From what Natwick told us, the Colombian syndicate is already involved. If MERGE truly has international power, I'd guess the Union de Corse is probably part of the organization, as well. The Corsican syndicate is an old ally of the Mafia, and it was barely scratched by the Executioner wars."

"Wait a minute," James began, "why would MERGE kill a U.S. congressman and an American diplomat?

After all, the mob has always steered clear of political assassinations—unless you believe some of the theories about JFK.''

''We may never know all the facts connected with the assassinations,'' Katz answered. ''But I suspect Franklin and Landers had probably threatened MERGE or failed to pay their cocaine suppliers because they assumed their connections with the U.S. government made them immune to retaliation.''

''From the beginning the assassinations seemed more like gangster hits than terrorist attacks,'' McCarter added as he steered the car onto Poinciana Drive. ''The killers took care not to harm innocent bystanders. They used subtle disguise instead of ski masks, and their methods were gangland style, as well. Brognola himself commented that using garlic on a knife blade was an old gangster trick.''

''By the way,'' James said. ''Speaking of Brognola, did you manage to get in touch with him to ask why he didn't fill us in on the fact Congressman Franklin was under investigation by the Congress as well as the Bahamian SIS?''

''Yes,'' Katz answered. ''Chock it up to computer malfunction. Hal couldn't be specific, but I gather that the Bear wasn't able to get a computer profile on Franklin or Landers because of a malfunction at the terminal tap to the memory banks of a personnel computer in Washington, D.C.''

''I wonder if that 'malfunction' was deliberate,'' the black man mused. ''And if it was, was it Washington or Stony Man that decided not to give us all the facts?''

''When you've worked for as many different intelligence organizations for as many years as I have,'' the

Israeli began with a wry grin, "you learn to accept the fact that you never know all the facts about a mission and you don't worry too much about it."

"Hell, yes," McCarter added. "When I was in the SAS you never knew who was lying to you. Military intel, SIS or the prime minister's office. That's part of how the game is played. If you get too paranoid you'll just worry yourself into an ulcer."

"Well, I suppose it's all water over the dam," James said with a shrug. "What do we do now?"

"We follow the same lead we had before," Katz replied. "Percy Haldren, the Black Angel."

"Nice idea," James agreed, gazing at the rows of towering apartment buildings and hotels that seemed to comprise half the structures in Nassau. "But where do we find the bastard? He sure as hell won't return to the Neptune's Palace."

"Haldren has probably headed to his spa in Andros," McCarter stated. "At least that's what Her Majesty's secret service figures."

"How the hell did you guys get information from British intelligence?" James asked with astonishment.

"Not too difficult, really." McCarter grinned. "After all, I am a British citizen, you know. I just headed to the embassy here in Nassau and convinced them to let me see the ambassador. Then we made an overseas phone call to my old mate Major Hillerman in Special Military Intelligence. You remember him when we had that little adventure in London a couple of months ago."

"Dude with the wooden leg," James said as he nodded. "You and he were in the SAS together during some campaign in Arabia."

"Oman, not Arabia," the Briton corrected. "Well, anyway, I said a couple of key phrases to let Hillerman know that Mark Daniels was really me. Hillerman then assured the ambassador that I was a trustworthy chap. After that, I was taken to meet the British SIS case officer operating in Nassau."

"British intelligence must be pretty active in the Bahamas," James commented.

"Have you been reading Ian Fleming again?" McCarter chuckled. "Seriously, British intelligence is fairly active in this area. Our chaps fit in pretty well here, and it's an ideal base of operations for keeping an eye on the Cubans and the Soviet activity in Central America. In the old days of the MI6, British agents used to meet with their CIA counterparts and compare notes in Nassau. Of course, that was before George Blake ruined the credibility of MI6, and the CIA became unable to keep state secrets. The two intel services don't trust each other much these days. Pity."

"Okay," James sighed. "But what's the British secret service interest in the Black Angel?"

"They were keeping tabs on Haldren because he was peddling cocaine to Congressman Franklin," McCarter explained. "In fact, the British SIS had already assumed the Angel had Franklin murdered. That's the reason they didn't get excited about the Bahamians Against Capitalist Oppression. They knew right away the BACO terrorists were a front for a criminal outfit of some sort, although I doubt they suspected anything as large as MERGE appears to be."

"Why didn't they share this information with the Bahamian SIS or the CIA?" James asked.

"Well, the British case officer didn't give me any details," McCarter answered. "But I suppose they didn't want to admit they've been spying on Congressman Franklin for some time before he was assassinated. Would be a bit embarrassing if they had to admit they knew all about Franklin's criminal activity in the Bahamas, but they never reported any of this to the Nassau authorities or the United States."

"But why were they keeping track of Franklin's high jinks and keeping it a secret from everybody else?" James inquired, an edge of frustration in his voice.

"Probably because Her Majesty's secret service intended to use the congressman themselves," the Briton said with a shrug.

"Wait a minute," the black man began. "I thought the United States and England were on the same side."

"Of course we are," McCarter assured him. "But we still spy on each other."

"Let me try to explain this, Calvin," Katz began. "The main commodity of value in the world of espionage and intelligence is information. When one acquires information by clandestine methods, one does not simply give it away. You might bargain it away, with either friend or foe, but you never just give it away. And if you can milk that source for more information, you damn well milk it dry."

"So the British were planning to blackmail Franklin into spying against the United States so he could act as a double agent for England?" James shook his head. "Man, that shit stinks."

"I doubt that the British would have tried to turn Franklin into a double agent," Katz replied.

"Of course not," McCarter added. "The bloke was unreliable. He was already a bloody security risk to the United States so SIS wouldn't trust him."

"True," the Israeli agreed. "I imagine they planned to keep collecting information on Franklin and the Angel until they had enough to make it worthwhile for dealing with Washington. Then they would have exchanged the data for other information more useful from London's point of view."

"You guys don't seem to see anything wrong with this sort of stuff," James said.

"When you were a cop didn't you use street informers in order to get information about criminals?" McCarter inquired.

"Sure," the ex-SWAT officer admitted.

"And weren't these informers usually criminals themselves?" the Briton continued. "But you didn't bust them because they could help you catch the bigger crooks. Well, the same thing is done in the world of espionage."

"Okay, I get your point," James said. "You mentioned that the Black Angel has a spa at someplace called Andros?"

"That's right," Katz answered. "Seems that Percy Haldren is into body building."

"Yeah," James said with a nod. "He sure looked like a weightlifter. Lots of muscle on that dude."

"Apparently the spa is Haldren's legal front for his income," the Israeli explained. "Technically he lives on the island of Andros, and he only comes to New Providence to do his banking and for recreation at the casinos."

"So when are we going to pay this spa a visit?" James asked eagerly.

"Gary and Rafael are waiting for us at a helicopter pad right now," Katz replied. "As soon as we're all together, we'll be ready to go."

10

Although Andros is the largest of the Bahamian islands, it is far less popular than New Providence or Grand Bahama. One of the Family Islands, formerly called the Out Islands, Andros does not appeal to tourists who favor gambling, tennis or golf. However, Andros is a fisherman's paradise. Amberjack, snapper and other fish can be found by the "Tongue of the Ocean," the second largest barrier reef in the world, which runs parallel to the east coast of Andros.

The adventurous are attracted to Andros. Swimming, snorkeling and spearfishing are among the favorite sports. Hunters stalk the forests in late autumn and the winter months. Treasure hunters still travel to North Andros in search of pirate loot at Morgan's Bluff. Legend has it Henry Morgan buried a treasure in this area, although none of it has ever been found.

Mysterious "Blue Holes" are located at several of the channels that run through most of Andros. A natural oddity, Blue Holes are fresh-water columns hundreds of feet deep. The best known of these is the Benjamin's Blue Hole, named in honor of Dr. George Benjamin who discovered stalagmites and stalactites more than a thousand feet under the sea. Such formations do not develop under water; thus, in 1967, Dr. Benjamin published his theory that the Bahamas are actually the tops of mountains, submerged for centuries under water.

Andros is a fascinating and exciting island, but it had not been the setting for a major battle since the days of the buccaneers. Nonetheless, Phoenix Force arrived at Andros Town, prepared for combat. The five men did not attract any special attention as they emerged from the transport chopper, carrying nylon suitcases and travel bags slung over their shoulders. They rented a Toyota Land Cruiser and embarked on the last leg of their journey before their showdown with the Black Angel.

Percy Haldren's spa, the Angel's Haven, was located seventy miles from Andros Town. The spa was too remote to be popular with tourists and, according to British SIS sources, Angel's Haven was closed to nonmembers, anyway. Phoenix Force was pleased by this news. They did not want innocent bystanders in the line of fire.

The five commandos easily followed a map, supplied by British intelligence, and soon caught sight of Haldren's lair. It was a handsome white building with Roman columns forming a porch-roof support. The rest of the spa was similar to a Southern plantation, except there was a large swimming pool in the rear, and the entire estate was surrounded by a twelve-foot-high iron fence.

"This is nice," Rafael Encizo remarked as he surveyed the place through a pair of Bushnell 7x50 binoculars. "There's a sign on the front gate that claims the spa is closed for repairs."

"Bloody good," McCarter agreed, unzipping his bag to remove a camouflage uniform and paratrooper boots. "That means nobody is home except the villains."

"What about security?" Katz inquired as he carefully slid his hooked prosthesis into the sleeve of a camou shirt. "Any alarms wired to that fence?"

"None that I've noticed," Encizo replied, still scanning the area with his field glasses. "There's a closed-circuit television camera mounted on a pine tree inside the fence. Fixed monitor system. Very standard. No guards, but I'm sure somebody is watching the monitors inside."

"Could be sound detectors or heat sensors," Gary Manning warned, as he also examined the spa through a pair of binoculars. "But I doubt it. I haven't found any kind of wiring hooked up to that fence, either."

"How we gonna handle this?" James inquired. He had changed into full camouflage uniform and buckled a gun belt around his narrow waist.

"We've got a pretty simple target," Katz replied with a shrug. "So let's just use the direct approach."

"Sounds fine to me," McCarter said cheerfully, as he examined his M-10 Ingram machine pistol. The Briton slid a 32-round magazine into the butt well and chambered the first cartridge.

"All right," the Israeli began. "Gary, can you get us through that fence without making too much noise?"

"Sure," Manning confirmed. The Canadian inserted shotgun shells into the extended tubular magazine of a Remington pump gun, modified with a SWAT-style folding stock.

"David, you take out the TV camera," Katz instructed. "Rafael and I will take point. Then David, Calvin and Gary take rear guard. Agreed?"

The others nodded.

"Now this is a simple assault," Katz stated as he gathered up his Uzi submachine gun, equipped with a foot-long silencer. "It's the sort of thing we've handled a dozen times before, and that's what worries me. It's the sort of assault that seems routine, but don't get cocky, and don't get careless."

"None of us figures we're taking on the Girl Scouts of America, Yakov," Calvin James assured him, unfolding the stock of his Smith & Wesson M-76 subgun.

"Then let's get to work," the Israeli declared.

McCarter moved forward alone, his camou-clad body blending with the tall grass surrounding the estate. He carried his Ingram slung over a shoulder and the Browning in shoulder leather in order to use both hands as he braced the skeletal stock of a Barnett Commando crossbow to his shoulder. McCarter peered through the telescopic sights until the cross hairs marked the surveillance camera mounted on the tree.

He squeezed the trigger. The bow string sang as it snapped forward to propel the bolt. The projectile shot between the bars of the fence and struck its target. Metal and plastic burst on impact. The lens popped from the camera, now worthless junk with the feathered shaft of the crossbow bolt jutting from its center.

Gary Manning hurried to the fence. The Canadian demolitions pro quickly placed a glob of puttylike substance at the base of two bars. He fitted a second charge at the brackets five feet from the ground. Manning carefully inserted two radio-receiver detonators and hastily joined the others.

The Canadian removed a special transmitter device and pressed the button. A low-wave radio signal triggered the detonators. The CV-38, a British low-velocity plastic explosive, erupted. The twin blasts blended to form a single sound that resembled a rather muffled version of a sonic boom.

The two bars burst from the fence, leaving a gap in the barrier roughly five feet high and a foot and a half wide. Katz handed his Uzi to Encizo as he approached the fence. The Israeli knelt by the gap and squeezed through to the other side.

"If I can make it," Yakov whispered, patting his slightly paunchy belly, "you guys shouldn't have any trouble at all."

Encizo slipped the Uzi through the bars to Katz. The Cuban then passed his own machine pistol, an H&K MP-5, to Yakov before he slithered through the gap to join the Israeli inside the enemy compound.

"Oh, shit!" a voice exclaimed. "Somebody is sneakin' in!"

Katz whirled, Uzi braced across his prosthesis. He spotted two men, both dressed casually in bush shirts and khaki shorts. One carried a walkie-talkie and a revolver holstered on his hip. The other guy was packing an M-3 submachine gun, pointed right at Katz and Encizo.

A bolt of movement suddenly cut through the air. The crossbow missile struck the machine gunner in the face. The man fell to his knees, the M-3 still in his fists. Six inches of fiberglass shaft with a feathered butt jutted from the gunner's right eye socket. The other eye was open wide, staring into the mysterious realm of death. He collapsed to the ground.

"Bull's-eye," McCarter whispered as he lowered his Barnett crossbow.

The other hoodlum tried to raise his walkie-talkie and

draw his pistol at the same time. He failed to accomplish either goal. Katz triggered his Uzi. The silenced subgun rasped harshly, firing a 3-round burst. A trio of 9mm slugs tore into the center of the thug's chest, chopping his heart and lungs to pieces.

"They must have come to check out the TV camera when it blinked out on the monitors inside," Encizo remarked. "Didn't waste much time, did they?"

"We'd better not, either," the Israeli stated.

Katz and Encizo headed for the spa as McCarter slipped through the gap in the fence. The Israeli and Cuban commandos approached a side entrance to the building. A heavyset thug appeared at the doorway, a sawed-off double-barrel shotgun in his hands.

Encizo's H&K coughed violently through the long steel sausage attached to its barrel. Parabellum missiles punched through flesh, forming a bloodied column of bullet holes from the guy's solar plexus to his throat. The gunman tumbled backward, his finger involuntarily pulling one of the scattergun triggers. A burst of buckshot exploded into the doorframe as the hood's corpse crashed to the floor.

The Cuban reached the door first. He dove headlong across the threshold and hit the floor in a smooth shoulder roll. A gunman, stationed in the hallway hastily fired his snub-nosed .38 at Encizo's tumbling form. The bullet missed and shrieked down the corridor until it buried itself in plaster.

The buttonman did not get a second chance. Katz poked his Uzi through the door and opened fire. A wave of 9mm rounds lifted the pistolman off his feet and hurled him into a corner. The hoodlum's bullet-ripped body slid to the floor.

The barrel of a CAR-15 auto-rifle shattered glass from a second-story window as McCarter raced toward the door. The Briton heard the crash of the windowpane above and glanced up to see flying glass and the metal rod of the rifle barrel. He immediately raised his Ingram and fired a full-auto salvo at the window.

A man's figure toppled forward. The remaining glass and framework gave way under the hoodlum's weight. His body plunged through the window and dived, almost gracefully, to the lawn below. Slashed by glass shards and torn by parabellum bullets, the blood-splashed corpse barely had enough muscular reflex left to manage a feeble twitch.

James and Manning rushed forward as McCarter bolted inside the spa. A pair of gun-toting thugs suddenly materialized from the back of the building. They swung their pistols at the black warrior and his Canadian comrade. Calvin James was faster. His S&W subgun raked the two hoods with an abrupt slash of 9mm hell.

One gunman was struck full in the face by two parabellums. The impact kicked him backward, and he stumbled dead on his feet. The corpse's shoe leather slipped on a damp spot near the pool, and the dead man fell into the water. His body floated to the surface, a dark liquid cloud forming around his shattered skull.

The other hoodlum caught a 9mm high in the left side of his chest and another bullet in the shoulder. The combined force of the slugs spun him around and he fell against an aluminum-and-plastic lawn chair by the pool. The wounded thug sat down hard, stunned and startled. Blood oozed from his bullet-torn flesh.

James and Manning had previously decided to attack

the spa from the rear so Phoenix Force could execute a more efficient two-prong strike. They jogged toward the pool. The wounded hoodlum, fearful that the commandos planned to finish him off, raised his pistol. Manning's shotgun bellowed. A blast of Number Four buckshot pulverized the guy's chest and knocked him backward in the lawn chair. The furniture tipped over, spilling the man's corpse to the tiles.

The Phoenix Force pair cautiously moved to the corner at the rear of the building. Manning pumped his Remington to eject the spent shell casing and chamber a fresh load of buckshot while James took the point. The black man held up a palm to urge Manning to stay where he was.

James had seen a shadow on the pavement. The outline of a head and shoulders told him someone was lurking around the corner. James pressed his back against the wall and slowly crept closer, breathing through his open mouth because even the sound of air passing through nostrils can betray a man's presence.

He waited. Seconds seem to become long minutes under stress. James reminded himself that the hoodlum around the corner had to wait just as long. The guy must be sweating it out just as bad, straining all his senses to try to determine if it was safe.

At last, a tawny-haired punk poked his head around the edge, a Luger pistol clenched in his sweaty little fist. James's left hand snaked out and snared the dude's wrist before he could use the German popgun.

The black badass rammed the muzzle of his M-76 into the kid's gut, knocking the wind from his opponent. He wrenched the captive wrist, forcing the punk to open his hand and drop the Luger. James pulled the dazed hood forward and shoved him toward Gary Manning. The kid hurled face first into the brawny Canadian's fist.

James whirled around the corner and triggered his S&W chatterbox, assuming that where you find one low-life, you generally find more. His theory proved sound. The volley of 9mm slugs ripped open a thug armed with an old Thompson subgun. The buttonman's body did a last tango of death and crashed into a patio table, snapping the stem of a canopy. The red-and-white umbrella fell on the corpse like a colorful shroud.

Manning grabbed the blond punk's face and slammed the back of his head into the wall. The kid sank to the ground, unconscious. Confident the young hoodlum would be out of action for at least half an hour, Manning hurried forward to join his partner.

Around the corner, they found a large set of sliding-glass doors. One door was open, inviting the Phoenix Force pair to enter. Sure, man, James thought. Come into my parlor. Fuck you, spider.

Gary Manning took a black canister from his belt and looked at James. The black man nodded approval when he recognized the device. Manning pulled the pin from the SAS "flash-bang" grenade. He held it for the count of three and lobbed the blaster through the open door.

Both men dashed around the corner and covered their ears. The concussion grenade exploded, shattering the glass doors, showering the patio with broken fragments. James and Manning rushed back to the entrance. The sliding doors had been virtually destroyed by the blast, and the pair stormed into the shambles that had formerly been a room.

It had been a gymnasium or a spa room or whatever the beautiful people liked to call a room where they worked out. All the fancy stuff was there, a Nautilis machine, an exercise bicycle, a couple of rowing devices and even a Jacuzzi in the center of the room. A mirror had covered one wall, but it had been destroyed by the blast of the concussion grenade.

Four groaning hoodlums sprawled on the floor, blood trickling from ruptured membranes in their nostrils and ears. James reached for the canvas medic's kit at the small of his back.

"I don't think you'd better patch these guys up right now," Manning advised.

"I'm just gonna give them some thorazine to make sure they don't go anywhere for a while," James answered.

"Okay," the Canadian agreed. "But...."

Manning saw one of the wounded hoodlums, sprawled behind a bicycle machine, suddenly sit up with a pistol in his fist. The Phoenix champ reacted instantly, pointing his Remington at the thug and opening fire. Buckshot smashed the exercise bike and slammed it into the gunman.

The hoodlum hardly noticed since other Number Four pellets had also split his skull open. He thrashed on the floor, embracing the bicycle. Man and machine became a single grotesque form, twisted, mangled and splattered with blood.

"I always wondered if you could get hurt on one of those things," James remarked, hoping his attempt at humor would conceal the fact that the unexpected shotgun blast had scared the hell out of him.

Manning prepared to jack a fresh shell into the breech of his Remington. His ears were still ringing from the effects of firing the shotgun in an enclosed area, so he did not hear the man splash about as he rose up from the water of the Jacuzzi.

The guy had been lucky. He had leaped into the miniature pool and been protected from the most violent effects of the concussion grenade. The thug had suffered a bloody nose and a few bruises, but he still had plenty of fight left as he leaped out of the pool and attacked Manning.

The Canadian sensed danger. He half turned as the hoodlum raced toward him. The Phoenix Force commando lifted his shotgun, holding it between his fists like a bar. The syndicate flunky twisted in midair and grabbed the frame of the Remington like an acrobat catching a trapeze.

However, Manning was also flexible in combat and able to flow from technique to technique as the situation demanded. He suddenly folded a leg and fell backward, pulling the hood forward. The Canadian's buttocks hit the floor. As he rolled back, Manning raised a boot to catch the attacker just above the belt. He pumped his leg and sent his opponent hurtling head-over-heels in a judo circle throw.

The hoodlum crashed to the floor hard, breath exploding from his stunned lungs. Manning sprang to his feet and rushed forward to render the punk unconscious with a blow from the metal stock of his shotgun, but the thug suddenly rolled over and slithered behind a rowing machine. Manning followed.

The thug rose, whirling a jumping rope over his head like the blades of a helicopter. A hard wooden handle cracked against Manning's skull, striking just above his left temple. The unexpected blow staggered the Canadian. The hood leaped over the rower and jumped Manning. This time both men fell to the floor. The shotgun skidded out of reach as the goon quickly wrapped the jump rope around Manning's neck.

Calvin James was about to help his partner when two men charged into the room. One was wiry with a swarthy goatlike face. The other was a mountain of black muscle with a Damballah snake charm hung around his neck. The Black Angel's eyes swelled as he recognized James.

"You!" Haldren snarled as he raised his Largo pistol.

But the goat-man was a greater threat at the moment because he held a sawed-off shotgun. James instinctively aimed and triggered the M-76, pumping two 9mm into the smaller man's face. The bullets burned through the gunman's brain and split open the back of his skull.

James held down the trigger as he swung the S&W subgun toward Haldren. The Black Angel was no combat pro. He was still fumbling with the safety catch as James pointed the M-76 at his chest.

Nothing happened.

The S&W had exhausted its magazine. James's fists tightened around the empty weapon. Haldren's broad face glowed as an evil smile bisected his dark features.

"Looks like you rolled the dice again," the Angel declared, aiming his Largo at James's face. "And lost."

11

Calvin James reacted with the speed and force of desperation. He suddenly hurled the empty M-76 at the Black Angel. The steel frame struck Haldren's fist, knocking the Largo autoloader from the big man's grasp. James immediately delivered a tae kwon-do side-kick to the Angel's midsection and snapped a fast backfist to his opponent's face.

Percy Haldren grabbed James's arm and hauled him forward. The muscular brute effortlessly flung the Phoenix Force warrior into the next room. James was unable to stop the increased momentum as he stumbled into the steel framework of a universal gym.

James whirled, clawing his Colt Commander from its hip holster. Haldren moved in fast. Powerful fingers seized James's wrist. The Angel's viselike grip forced James's fist to open, dropping the .45 pistol. Haldren kicked the gun across the floor. James lashed his left fist into the giant's grinning face. His knuckles stung from the impact, but the Black Angel still smiled.

Haldren swung a left hook to James's jaw. The blow sent him tumbling over the bench built into the chest-press portion of the universal gym. James hit the floor hard, lights popping painfully inside his aching head.

"No wonder the Americans laugh at their niggers,"

Haldren snorted. "Get up! Let's see what you're made of."

James gazed up at the Black Angel. Haldren towered over him, gesturing with wiggling fingers, a mocking smile still plastered across his billboard face. Calvin James rose to his feet, determined to wipe that goddamn grin off his opponent's smug features.

"You're real tough when you're beating up women, asshole," he sneered as he assumed a T-dachi stance.

"You Yanks have an expression," Haldren remarked, dropping his hands to his sides. "Give it your best shot, boy."

James cocked back his right fist as if prepared to swing a wild right cross. Suddenly he pivoted and leaped into the air. His right leg whirled around like an Olympic hammer. The back of his heel crashed into the side of Percy Haldren's face with enough force to break a house brick.

The Angel's head jerked from the powerful kick. He no longer smiled as he rolled his tongue inside his mouth and glared at Calvin James. Then he spat on the floor. A broken tooth bounced off the wooden surface.

"Not bad," Haldren said with a grin.

"Oh, shit," James rasped as he bolted away from the monstrous juggernaut.

James ran to a pommel horse at the opposite end of the gym. He hastily grabbed the handles and vaulted over the coup as the Black Angel charged after him. James shuffled to the neck of the horse, keeping the Nissen gymnastic device between Haldren and himself.

"Come now, boy," the Angel scoffed as he rushed forward and swung a punch at James's head. The Phoenix pro ducked and slithered to the other end of the horse. "This isn't fighting."

James glanced around the gym. It was an iron room, equipped with barbells, dumbbells and weights, as well as the universal gym in the center of the room. A heavy body bag, used by boxers to develop punching power, hung from thick chains attached to the ceiling.

"Run out of karate tricks, boy?" Haldren chuckled. "Want to learn some new tricks, eh?"

He gripped the body of the horse with one hand and an upright with the other and suddenly shoved the Nissen. It tipped forward on its base and tumbled upside down. Haldren laughed as he reached for Calvin James with both hands, planning to tear him apart like an insect.

GARY MANNING COULD NOT BREATHE. His opponent had pinned him to the floor, holding down the Canadian's arms under his knees as he continued to throttle Manning with the jump-rope garrote. The Canadian tried to get proper leverage to topple the hoodlum, but the thug simply leaned forward and pulled the rope harder.

The constriction at Manning's throat had cut off his carotid arteries. His eyesight was becoming dim and consciousness threatened to slip away at any second. His fingers raked the floor. Something sharp pricked his thumb. Manning grasped the object, realizing it was a large sliver of broken glass.

Survival would depend on doing the right thing and doing it fast. Manning quickly bent a knee and whipped it up to strike his tormentor in the kidney. The man groaned and his body shifted. His knee slipped from Manning's right forearm.

The Canadian immediately thrust the glass sliver at his opponent's torso. It pierced under the man's rib cage, stabbing deep. The hoodlum shrieked and released the rope. Manning's fist slammed into his face, knocking the aggressor off his chest.

The Phoenix Force champ crawled to his stunned adversary and punched him again. Blood dribbled from the guy's split lip as Manning grabbed the thug's hair with one hand and seized his jaw with the other. The Canadian pulled with one arm and pushed with the other, violently twisting the man's head. Vertebrae snapped.

Manning had broken the thug's neck.

He removed the jump rope from his own neck and gulped air into his tortured lungs. Manning slowly got to his feet, shaking his head to clear it. A door suddenly burst open, and Manning yanked an S&W .41 Magnum from his hip holster.

"Easy, Gary," a familiar voice urged. Colonel Katzenelenbogen stepped across the threshold, his Uzi canted on a shoulder, barrel pointing toward the ceiling. "Only friendly forces left."

"Thank God," the Canadian said with a sigh as he lowered his revolver. "Anybody hurt?"

"None of our side got so much as a scratch," Katz replied. "Except you. Maybe you'd better sit down and wait for Calvin to take a look at you."

"Calvin." Manning's eyes widened. "Where is Calvin?"

THE BLACK ANGEL leaped back to avoid the flashing steel in Calvin James's fist. The Phoenix fighter had managed to draw a G-96 Jet-Aer dagger from his belt sheath. Now it was Percy Haldren's turn to retreat. The Angel backed up, holding his arms ready to guard against James's knife.

"I thought this was supposed to be a fair fight," Haldren complained, eyes locked on the G-96.

"So sue me," James replied as he suddenly tossed the knife from his right hand to the left.

The black commando's arm struck out fast. Haldren yelped as the blade slashed the back of his right hand. Blood dripped from the shallow wound as the Angel ran to the body bag and ducked behind it for cover.

James dashed forward and leaped toward the bag, his body canted in midair, right leg extended. His boot slammed into the bag, driving it backward to smack into Haldren's torso. The Black Angel groaned and fell backward against a wall. James moved in for the kill.

Haldren suddenly slapped both hands across the bag, swinging it into James. The Phoenix Force crusader was knocked off his feet. The blow pitched him four feet and he landed on his ass, pain shooting up from his tailbone. James glanced up and saw the haft of his dagger protruding from the body bag. The blade was buried in the canvas. Sand bled onto the floor beneath it.

"No rules, eh?" the Black Angel said with a smile as he pulled the knife from the bag. "That's fine with me, boy."

Calvin James scrambled to his feet and dashed back to the universal gym. Haldren darted after him and lunged with the knife, aiming for the commando's back. James jumped onto the bench press and leaped up to the top of the gym, his feet slipping on the skeletal frame as he scrambled up. Haldren slashed the Jet-Aer dagger at James's legs, hoping to severe an Achilles tendon. The commando bounded to the top of the gym, barely avoiding the lashing blade.

Haldren attempted to climb the steel framework, but his muscle-bound body was neither quick nor agile. The Angel reached the top and slashed the knife again. James slithered across the narrow bars to dodge the dagger. Sparks erupted when steel struck steel, and the blade snapped off at the tang. Haldren cursed and tossed the useless knife handle aside.

The Black Angel jumped down from the gym and ran around to the other side, hoping to reach James from a different angle. The Phoenix Force battle pro dived from the top and seized the chinning-bar section of the universal gym. He swung toward Haldren and raised his knees to drive the heels of both feet into the Angel's face. The powerful kick sent Haldren reeling. The brute fell to the floor, blood pouring from his pulverized mouth.

Calvin James jumped down from the chinning bar and dashed to an assortment of barbells, dumbbells and weight plates. Haldren rose up from the floor, snarling with rage as he launched himself at the commando. James grabbed a dumbbell with fifty pounds of weight plates bolted to the short bar. He raised the dumbbell in both fists as Haldren advanced, arms spread and fingers arched like claws. James rushed forward and swung the weight set with all his might.

The dumbbell crashed into the top of Percy Haldren's skull. Bone cracked open and blood streamed down the Black Angel's forehead. The great beast collapsed at James's feet. Calvin James raised the dumbbell and smashed it into Haldren's head again. Blood and brains splashed the commando's shirt sleeves.

"Holy shit!" Gary Manning exclaimed as he and Yakov Katzenelenbogen rushed into the iron room to find their partner kneeling beside the twitching remains of the Black Angel.

"Didn't..." James stammered, panting hard from exhaustion and stress. "Didn't you ever...see a dude... work out in a gym...before?"

12

"I talked to the chief of police of Andros Town," Major Alby said wearily. "He isn't very happy about that collection of dead bodies you left at Angel's Haven."

"Figure we should have buried them?" Calvin James inquired as he inspected the mouthpiece and hose to an Emerson diver's tank.

Phoenix Force had returned from Andros and headed back to the warehouse safe base at the outskirts of Nassau. The five-man army reported briefly to Alby. The SIS officer had listened with his mouth hanging open in astonishment. Then he hurried to a telephone and contacted the authorities in Andros.

"You men have only been in the Bahamas for forty-eight hours," Alby said with a sigh. "And I've already lost count of the number of bodies that have popped up."

"There will probably be a few more before this is over," Rafael Encizo commented as he checked a diver's face mask to be certain the lens was not cracked.

"What are you planning to do with that diving gear?" Alby inquired.

"Water sports," the Cuban replied with a grin, examining a powerful CO_2 Strebling speargun.

"The major deserves a better answer than that," Yakov Katzenelenbogen began. "We searched the slain enemies and discovered several carried membership identification for the Third Chapter of the Lucayan Stevedores' United. Taking a look at a map of the Bahamas, we found that Lucaya Bay is located on the coast of Grand Bahama."

"It's near Freeport," Alby confirmed. "And I've heard of the Lucayan Stevedores' United before. It was under investigation last year. One or two chapters were accused of involvement in a drug-smuggling operation."

"Cocaine from Colombia?" Gary Manning asked.

"That's right," the major responded. "How did you guess?"

"Some of the flunkies at Angel's Haven were actually dumb enough to carry Colombian passports," the Canadian replied. "More evidence that the Colombian Syndicate is associated with MERGE."

"Well, the investigation of the Lucayan Stevedores' United didn't get too far," Alby explained. "The other stevedore unions started to cry about harassment before they knew any of the details. Labor has a lot of pull in parliament, so the government called off the investigation when it started stepping on a few union bosses' toes."

"Is there any way you can find out who heads the Third Chapter of the Stevedores' United?" Katz inquired.

"Certainly," the major replied. "But what are you planning to do?"

"Go to Grand Bahama," Katz answered. "There's obviously a connection between the terrorists and the stevedores' union. At least among the members of the Third Chapter."

"And for so many MERGE thugs to be connected with

that chapter," McCarter added as he attached a sound suppressor to the threaded barrel of his M-10 Ingram, "it suggests the bloke in charge is probably a villain, as well."

"I suppose that makes sense," Alby agreed. "I was certainly wrong when I thought you chaps would just go through the motions to cover up for CIA misconduct."

"That's understandable, considering the corrupt nature of Fred Landers and Congressman Franklin," Manning assured him. "Sometimes it can be difficult to tell the good guys from the bad guys."

"You fellows seem to be able to figure that out, all right," Alby remarked. "But I think I'd better go with you to Grand Bahama. I can contact our SIS people there and see what information they have on the Stevedores' United."

"We'd appreciate that, Major," Katz replied.

"Good," Alby said. "Then I'd better get packed. Should I draw a submachine gun from our special weapons department?"

"Only if you know how to use it," James told him. "And you've been trained to handle commando-style assaults."

"As a matter of fact," the major began with a smile, "we've been concerned about the possibility of terrorist activity in the Bahamas for the past ten years. So many wealthy Americans, British and Western Europeans come here each year we had to consider the possibility that some radical group might attempt a kidnapping or assassination. The Bahamian government hired experts in antiterrorism, including authorities from the United States, Great Britain and West Germany. I've received quite a bit of training in such tactics."

"Have you got any *real* experience?" McCarter asked.

"Not yet," Alby admitted. "But I'll do exactly what you tell me to do."

"What if we tell you you can't go into combat?" Katz inquired.

"Then I'll obey orders," the major agreed. "But I want to participate. After all, the Bahamas is my home."

"I understand," Katz said. "But you don't have to wield a gun to serve your country."

"But if I can help?" Alby asked hopefully.

"We'll see," the Israeli replied.

DON FAZZIO ONCE AGAIN sat at the head of the conference table to meet with his fellow comrades of MERGE. The don's expression was grim, his eyes as hard as tempered steel. Henri LeTrec took a cigarette from a gold pocket case and fired the end. Juan Vargas smiled as he watched the fish tank. One of the piranha had been bitten by his brethren during a feeding frenzy. The other fish had turned on the wounded piranha, attracted by blood.

The price for carelessness, the Mexican Mafia ringleader thought as the fish tore the injured piranha to pieces.

Raul Ortega did not smile. He chewed the butt of a Havana cigar as he glanced from face to face. Ortega did not want to look at them, but he had to. To avoid their eyes would be admitting fear. To stare might be considered arrogant. Ortega could not afford to exhibit either emotion.

"I'm not going to mince words," Don Fazzio announced. "We're all aware of what has happened over the past two days. Our front operation at the Neptune's

Palace has been ruined. Salvadore Conti and several other good men were killed. Then, earlier today, Angel's Haven was attacked. Although all branches of MERGE were involved with these operations, both were part of the cocaine traffic that is spearheaded by Señor Ortega. The same Señor Ortega who, at our last meeting, assured us that the assassination of a United States congressman wouldn't cause MERGE any problems."

"And what does Señor Ortega have to say about this matter?" LeTrec inquired, blowing a smoke ring at the ceiling.

"I must admit that this situation does not look good," the Colombian began. "But it is not as bad as it appears. The blame is not mine. Percy Haldren was the target of these attackers."

"Haldren was one of your lieutenants, correct?" Fazzio asked. "The one known as the Black Angel?"

"Haldren was very useful," Ortega insisted. "He ran a large loan-shark operation, the largest in the Bahamas, even before I enlisted him into the service of MERGE. Many of our Bahamian contract men were soldiers in Haldren's operation."

"But Haldren is dead," LeTrec commented. "And you're still alive, señor."

"The police did not raid the Neptune's Palace or the Angel's Haven," Ortega declared. "No one was arrested. Whoever attacked these sites did so in a most ruthless manner. Dozens were killed. The others are missing, apparently abducted."

"What's your point?" Fazzio asked with a shrug.

"I think Haldren and his operations were attacked by some sort of competition group," Ortega answered. "Probably a paramilitary group. The gunmen were very skilled and well armed. Whoever they are, they are very professional."

"Paramilitary?" Fazzio frowned.

"The assault on the spa best proves this," the Colombian explained. "Crossbows and silenced weapons were used. Explosives were also involved, and what little evidence I've gotten from informers in the Andros police department indicates the invaders were armed with nine-millimeter machine pistols and a 12-gauge shotgun. With the lack of numerous bullet holes in walls and such, we can assume these gunmen are superb marksmen."

"How many men were in this mystery assault force?" Fazzio demanded, a trace of urgency in his voice.

"The police are not sure yet," Ortega replied. "From the bootprints left on the ground, the police believe there were more than four men but fewer than eight. Probably only five or six."

"You mean they purposely attacked a base where the odds were greater than two against one?" LeTrec asked.

"Some men will tackle odds far greater than that," Fazzio said grimly. "It depends on the man. Sometimes one man against a hundred is even odds."

"Cristo," Juan Vargas muttered. "You are talking about the Executioner, no? Bolan is dead, Don Fazzio."

"Of course." Fazzio nodded, although he felt the icy feet of a centipede of fear run up his spine. "But what are we talking about? A team of professional mercenaries, perhaps?"

"Probably," Ortega replied. "Of course, the question is, who hired them?"

"CIA?" LeTrec suggested. "It would not be the first time the Company hired soldiers of fortune to do their dirty work."

"You worry too much about the gringo CIA," Vargas sneered. "They're too scared of the *norteamericano* press to do anything. Since all gringos like to be on television, they're willing to tell all about any sort of spy activity they can find out about. Newspaper writers, TV reporters, congressmen who care more about media coverage than national security and even some of the spies themselves, all are willing to make CIA secrets public headlines so they can be famous on television."

"But this has all happened since Congressman Franklin was killed," Fazzio said.

"That doesn't prove the CIA is involved," Ortega replied. "But it suggests someone who knew about Haldren did this. Someone, perhaps, who also knows about MERGE and wants to cause trouble within our organization."

"You making an accusation?" Vargas asked tensely. "Make it so everybody understands, Ortega."

"Not an accusation," the Colombian began. "Just an observation. Members of your Mexican mafia are here on the islands, but so far there has been little use for them in the Bahamas. Since you are obviously low man on the totem pole, perhaps you plan to climb higher by—"

Juan Vargas stood up quickly, knocking over his chair. The Mexican glared at Ortega, his fists clenched with rage. Don Fazzio hastily rapped his knuckles on the table to call them to order before violence erupted.

"Señor Vargas, please sit down," the don said sharply. "And, Ortega, your remark was out of line unless you back it up with something besides your fuckin' mouth."

Fazzio was angry. *Very* angry. His polite veneer had melted away, and he was talking like a street hood. That was a bad sign. Ortega realized this anger was directed at him.

"My apologies, Don Fazzio," the Colombian said quickly. "I meant no offense, but...."

"I warned you before that MERGE wouldn't take the fall for you, Ortega," the don snapped. "Any way you cut it, this is your mistake."

"What do you want me to do, Don Fazzio?" Ortega asked quietly.

"That isn't the question anymore," Fazzio stated. "The question is, what are we going to do with you?"

"Don Fazzio," LeTrec began, "before we decide on any rash actions, may I suggest that Señor Ortega personally handles the delivery of heroin arriving from France tonight?"

"What if these mystery commandos show up there, as well?" Vargas inquired.

"That's why I think Ortega should handle it," LeTrec said, smiling. "If they attack the harbor, then Ortega gets blamed. The Colombian syndicate takes the fall, but the rest of MERGE won't be touched. However, if everything goes smoothly, then Ortega will have proven his ability to a degree, and we can reconsider his future position with the organization."

"All right," the don agreed. "But you'd better understand something, Ortega. This is your last chance. Fuck up again and I'll have your head. I mean that *literally*, pal. I'll have your head chopped off so I can feed it to my fish."

"I understand, Don Fazzio," Ortega assured him.

"And don't get any ideas about trying to run," the don added. "MERGE is everywhere."

"I know, Don Fazzio," Ortega replied. "I know."

13

Paul Wainwright sipped his Scotch and tonic as he gazed out the window of his penthouse apartment on Royal Palm Way. Below him, the city of Freeport was ablaze with street lamps and neon lights. Hotels and resorts were everywhere, some featuring Islamic teardrop domes and minarets to resemble sultans' palaces.

The entire west coast of Grand Bahama is geared for the tourist trade, Wainwright thought, offering everything from gambling at El Casino to shopping at the International Bazaar.

But once upon a time Grand Bahama was a haven for smugglers and cutthroats. It had once been an island of pirates and buccaneers. During the years of Prohibition in the United States, Grand Bahama was a notorious headquarters for bootleggers and rum runners. Paul Wainwright's grandfather had been involved in the illegal booze business and his father was a gunrunner during the 1950s, selling weapons to various revolutionary groups in Central America with little regard to their politics or morality.

Wainwright saw himself as merely carrying on the family tradition. He had long ago seen the advantages of controlling a stevedore-union chapter, and had worked long and hard to achieve his goal. After weeding out the more principled members of the chapter, Wainwright had turned the stevedores into an organized band of smugglers who could operate without suspicion as they loaded and unloaded ships docked at Hermit Harbor.

Well, almost without suspicion. The government had poked about for a while, but they had backed off before they could prove the Third Chapter was involved in the cocaine trade. Nonetheless, the experience had shattered Wainwright's nerves. He had been afraid to join forces with MERGE, but the Colombian syndicate knew too much about him. The scum threatened to turn him over to the authorities unless he agreed to work for MERGE.

Wainwright had considered fleeing the country, but the tentacles of MERGE were everywhere. The United States, Central and South America, Western Europe—MERGE would find him regardless of where he fled.

He finished his Scotch and turned away from the window. Wainwright gasped when he saw two men dressed in black clothing. The glass slipped from his fingers and shattered on the polished mahogany floor.

"Good evening, Mr. Wainwright," Yakov Katzenelenbogen greeted him, executing a mock salute with the steel hooks of his prosthesis. "Sorry to startle you."

"Yeah," Rafael Encizo added as he returned a set of lock picks to a leather pouch and slipped them into his pocket. "Wouldn't want you to have a heart attack. Not yet, anyway."

"Who are you?" Wainwright asked, his voice strained with terror.

"That doesn't matter," Katz replied simply. "All you need to know is we expect some answers to some very important questions. If you fail to answer us, we'll be forced to kill you."

Wainwright bolted for his desk, desperate to get his

H&K 9mm pistol from the top right-hand drawer. Katz almost casually raised his left arm and aimed a SIG-Sauer P-226 combat pistol. The Israeli squeezed the trigger. A parabellum slug hissed from a nine-inch silencer and smacked into the backrest of a leather armchair behind the desk.

The bullet split upholstery and splintered the wooden slat at the back of the chair. Wainwright jumped back from the desk, his mouth open, about to cry out in fear. Encizo suddenly seized the Bahamian and abruptly twisted Wainwright's right arm behind his back and simultaneously clamped a hand over the guy's mouth.

"Don't get cute, hombre," the Cuban whispered. "I'm going to cuff you now. Put your hands behind your back. Try any tricks and I'll bounce your face off the top of that desk. Even if you get away from me, my friend will put a bullet in your kneecap before you get three feet."

"All right," Wainwright mumbled through Encizo's palm. "No need to get rough."

"A civilized man," Katz mused. "How refreshing."

Encizo bound Wainwright's wrists together with unbreakable plastic riot cuffs. The Cuban quickly but professionally patted down the Bahamian for hidden weapons. Satisfied, Encizo hauled Wainwright to a large chocolate-brown leather sofa.

"He's clean," the Cuban announced as he shoved Wainwright into the couch.

"Good," the Israeli said, lowering his SIG-Sauer. "Now we can all relax a bit."

"Look," Wainwright began in a shaky voice, "I don't know what you men want...."

"Then shut up and listen," Encizo said sharply.

"You have a nice apartment, Wainwright," Katz remarked, glancing about the penthouse. "Must be very expensive. What's your rent here? Two thousand a month?"

"Two thousand five hundred," Wainwright answered.

"That's pretty good for a minor union official," Katz commented as he sat in an armchair across from the terrified Bahamian. "Do you sell greeting cards on the side?"

"You're not tax collectors," Wainwright said. "I don't have to answer any questions!"

The silenced SIG-Sauer coughed. A 9mm bullet punched the leather on the backrest of the couch, inches from Wainwright's right elbow. He yelped fearfully and jumped to his feet. Encizo pushed a hand to the guy's shoulder and shoved him back to the couch.

"You'd better be concerned with your survival, Wainwright," Katz warned. "We're not murderers. We don't want to kill you, but we will if we have to. You see, Mr. Wainwright, this is a war. You probably regard your activities as a business venture, but we're at war. At the moment, we're on opposite sides. You can either defect or die."

"Who are you?" Wainwright asked.

"We're not the police or the SIS or the CIA or any other organization you're familiar with," the Israeli explained. "In other words, we don't have to answer to anyone. We can kill you right here and now. No one will ever know we did it. No one will even ask us if we were involved."

"But I'm just the president of the Third Chapter of the Stevedores' United," Wainwright stated. "I'm not some sort of supercrook or master spy or whatever you think I am.''

"Let's save some time," Katz began. "We know about MERGE and we know that many members of your union chapter are members of MERGE, or at least contract gunmen working for the organization. We've also done some checking and we've discovered that your chapter of the Stevedores' United was suspected of cocaine smuggling a while back.''

"All charges were dropped," Wainwright said.

"The investigation was terminated because of politics," Encizo commented. "That doesn't prove you people were guilty, but it doesn't make you innocent, either.''

"You've no right to pass judgment on me," Wainwright insisted. "This is vigilante behavior!"

"Suddenly you're concerned with justice," Katz said as he laughed. "You've been involved with smuggling illegal narcotics, associated with a criminal organization that has people abducted, beaten and murdered. But now you're expecting us to respect your rights. That really is amusing, Mr. Wainwright.''

"Yeah," Encizo added, drawing his Gerber Mark I combat dagger from its belt sheath. "Somebody might just die laughing before this is over.''

"Mr. Wainwright," Katz continued, "we know about MERGE, and we know about your smuggling operations. A computer check confirmed that virtually all the stevedores in your union chapter have criminal records. Most of them are foreigners from the United States, Bermuda, Central America. We checked with Interpol and discovered that every one of them is wanted for crimes committed in their own countries and they're using false names here in the Bahamas.''

"Which means they'll be deported," Encizo remarked. "We also found out that the Third Chapter handles cargo exclusively for Hermit Harbor. Taking a look at the ships bringing imports, they all seem to be from Mexico or Colombia. Marijuana and cocaine, right?"

"That's not true," Wainwright said helplessly.

"And your exports are mostly to the United States," Katz stated. "It's a long way around to deliver narcotics to the U.S., but it also reduces the odds of being discovered by customs."

"MERGE is a pretty shrewd outfit," Encizo commented. "And it must be pretty big, too. We understand some remnants of the Mafia, the Colombian syndicate and probably the Mexican Mafia are connected to MERGE."

"We also discovered that a ship from France called *Le Monarque* is due to arrive tonight," Katz declared. "And considering what we already know about MERGE, we suspect the Corsican syndicate is also part of the organization. This suggests the cargo on *Le Monarque* is almost certainly heroin."

"That's absurd," Wainwright stammered.

"Well, we'll find out soon enough," Katz said. "You see, the Bahamian SIS, the customs department and the Bahamian Coastal Patrol are going to join us when we inspect *Le Monarque*, and I'm sure we'll find the heroin."

"Then what do you need me for?" Wainwright asked, fearful of the answer.

"If you tell us where the heroin is hidden," Encizo began, "it will save us a lot of time and effort. And it will prove that you're willing to cooperate with us. This means we can make a deal for you to turn state's witness and charges against you will be reduced. You'll be protected from MERGE.''

"Protected?" Wainwright glared at the Cuban. "How do you intend to protect me from MERGE? They have agents planted in every major police department in the Bahamas!"

Wainwright gasped, suddenly aware that he had blurted his knowledge about the criminal network. He shook his head with dismay, drained of energy.

"I won't go to court," Wainwright declared. "I'll never confess to any of this under oath."

"We'll talk about that later," Katz replied. "Right now, you'd better understand something. MERGE isn't as great a threat to you as we are at this moment. You can either give us some information or Mr. Rodriguez will try to convince you to cooperate."

Encizo leaned forward and held his knife in front of Wainwright's face. He slowly lowered the Gerber and deftly flicked his wrist. The blade popped a button from the Bahamian's silk shirt.

"What do you want to know?" Wainwright asked, almost sobbing with fear.

"How well armed are those hoods in your union chapter, and how many of them will be at the pier?"

"Mostly shotguns and a few handguns," Wainwright answered. "They don't keep full-auto weapons at the dock in case the police get curious. There should be at least a dozen men present to unload the shipment."

"Any idea how many Corsicans will be on *Le Monarque*?" the Israeli inquired.

"The ship is owned and operated by the Corsican syndicate," Wainwright conceded. "As far as I know, everyone from the captain to the ship's cook will be a member of the syndicate. I don't know how well armed they'll be, but I assume they have a cache of weapons onboard. The heroin is being transported inside a bronze elephant.''

"An elephant?'' Encizo frowned. "The entire heroin stash is inside a single statue of an elephant?''

"The statue is life size,'' Wainwright explained. "In order to get to the heroin, one has to burn through the bronze with a blow torch.''

"Very clever,'' the Cuban was forced to admit. "An elephant full of dope. It sounds so silly no one would suspect it.''

"That's what MERGE is counting on,'' Wainwright confirmed. "Now, do you want to know where you can find Don Antonio Fazzio?''

"Who, or should I say *what*, is Don Antonio Fazzio?'' Katz asked.

"He's more or less the top man of MERGE operations in the Bahamas,'' Wainwright answered. If he'd come this far he might as well go all the way. "He has a fortress on an island located along the Exuma Sound, about a hundred miles from the coast of San Salvador.''

"Oh, yes,'' Katz replied. "We'd be delighted to hear about that, but first we've got a ship to catch.''

14

"Oh, shit," Calvin James muttered as he gazed through a Starlite viewer, adjusting the light-density level to turn the darkness of midnight to twilight. "*Le Monarque* has already arrived."

Phoenix Force, Major Alby and Special Investigator Heywood of the customs department were positioned on a rooftop three blocks from Hermit Harbor. A two-hundred-foot-long cargo ship had docked in the harbor. Sailors aboard the vessel pulled a canvas tarp from a huge hump-backed figure. It was a bronze statue of an African elephant, trunk curled back to its massive brow, metal tusks pointing at the night sky.

"It would have been a lot easier if we could have taken out the stevedores first and then dealt with the Corsicans when the ship arrived," Gary Manning said with a sigh. "Now we'll have to take 'em all on at once. How many do you think are down there, Mr. Scott?"

"Oh," James said with a shrug, "about thirty or thirty-five guys and one brass elephant."

"Bronze," Encizo said with a grin. "Let's stick with the facts, amigo."

"The only fact I need to know is: that big sucker is full of heroin," James whispered through clenched teeth. "That's enough to make me want to blow all those dudes away and send that metal Jumbo to the Elephants' Graveyard, man.''

The black warrior had a special reason for hating heroin and anyone who sold it. His younger sister had died from an overdose of horse and his mother was murdered, almost certainly by dope addicts. James eagerly loaded his M-76 subgun and two M-26 fragmentation grenades into a thick rubber bag and snapped the seal shut.

"Look at those crazy bastards trying to move that statue across the deck," David McCarter said with a smile, as he watched several stevedores and sailors struggle with the elephant.

"This whole business is crazy," Manning said. "Hauling dope all the way from France hidden inside a bronze elephant. Looks like they're preparing for a Republican convention down there."

"What do you want?" McCarter grinned. "A metal donkey? Or maybe a Canadian moose, eh?"

"They're crazy as a fox," Encizo remarked. "If we didn't know what was inside that elephant, we'd assume it was just an unusually large statue on its way to a museum or a zoo."

"What worries me is the number of villains down there," Inspector Heywood confessed. "You know I've only brought three men with me. We're customs inspectors, not commandos. You should have gotten the narcotics people instead. The United States and Britain have agents stationed in Nassau, you know."

"We couldn't convince them we were serious," Major Alby explained. "When I told them about an elephant full of heroin they hung up on me. One of the Yanks asked me if the elephant was polka dotted or just pink."

"How many SIS agents are present?" Heywood asked.

"Five," Alby replied. "But only two of them have received training in commando tactics and counterterrorism. However, there are two Coastal Patrol boats waiting for a signal to swoop down on Hermit Harbor. The patrols are armed with pump shotguns and Browning automatics."

"Well, those blokes will take about half an hour to move that bleedin' elephant," McCarter commented as he chambered a round into the breech of his Ingram machine pistol. "We'd damn well better be in position by then."

"We go to Plan B," Katz, the master strategist, announced. "My people know what to do. We'll go in first. Major, you'll head the second team. Don't advance until the shooting starts."

"Wait a minute," Heywood began. "I thought we were going to arrest these chaps. You talk as if you intend to simply gun them down."

"When we're in position we'll signal you, and you can order the gangsters to surrender," Katz replied. "But do it from a bullhorn and stay out of range and under cover because I guarantee they'll start shooting. The goons in Wainwright's union might be willing to surrender, but the Corsicans will certainly put up a fight."

"You customs blokes just stay the hell out until we've got the situation under control," McCarter stated. "You'll just get in the way during a firefight."

"Right," Katz agreed. "The same goes for the SIS who haven't been trained for counterterrorism. They can man the radios and keep in contact with the Freeport police. It's vital that the police keep this area blocked off so civilian motorists and pedestrians don't stumble upon the battlefield. Stopping that heroin is important, but it isn't more important than the lives of innocent bystanders."

"We also want to reduce the likelihood of casualties among our own forces," Encizo commented as he slipped three star-shaped metal objects into a pouch on his weight belt.

The Cuban and Calvin James wore black wetsuits. They strapped on Emerson tanks and pulled on diving masks. The other members of Phoenix Force wore black night camouflage uniforms. Alby and some of his SIS agents had also donned dark clothing for the occasion. Heywood and his customs men had displayed their ignorance of the situation by wearing business suits and ties. The only weapons the customs agents carried were small-caliber pistols.

"Give us enough time to soften the bastards up before the rest of you move in," Katz reminded Alby. "And don't forget to use the gas grenades, and don't fire at anyone unless you're sure he's the enemy. None of these hoods are key figures in MERGE, so if one or two manage to escape it's not a big deal. We can always catch them later. Any questions?"

No one responded. The time for talk was over. It was now time for action.

TWO STEVEDORES STOOD in front of the warehouse. They smoked cigarettes and glanced about at the other buildings by the harbor. Neither man appeared to be armed.

Gary Manning peered through the infrared scope mounted to his Anschultz .22-caliber air rifle. The Canadian gently squeezed the trigger. The Anschultz hissed as a steel dart catapulted from its barrel. One of the sentries yelped with pain as the needle point pierced the side of his neck.

The sentry slapped at the hornet sting. He pulled the dart from his neck and examined it with surprise. His partner asked what was wrong. The first guard opened his mouth to reply when two hundred milligrams of thorazine took effect. The guy's eyes rolled toward the sky and he passed out.

The first sentry slumped unconscious. His startled comrade reached inside his Windbreaker for a snub-nosed revolver. David McCarter triggered his Barnett Commando crossbow. A steel-tipped bolt slashed through the darkness. The sharp tip punctured the second sentry's heart. Cyanide seeped from the slit in the fiberglass shaft. The guard died so quickly he did not even have time to groan.

Manning, McCarter and Katz emerged from the shadows. The Canadian warrior headed around the side of the building, Remington riot shotgun slung over a shoulder and a backpack full of explosives hung between his shoulder blades. McCarter moved to the opposite side of the warehouse, armed with his M-10 Ingram. Katz stationed himself at the front of the building and crouched by the door, Uzi braced across his prosthetic right arm.

Manning carefully placed a four-ounce packet of CV-38 at a windowsill, then the Canadian demolitions expert crept to the rear of the building and took a radio transmitter from his pocket. He pressed a button and detonated the gray putty explosive.

The low-velocity blast shattered the window and ripped out the flimsy framework. The explosion was a signal to Katz and McCarter. The Israeli and British commandos both pulled pins from SAS concussion grenades and lobbed the blasters through windows. The "flash-bang" grenades exploded in unison, causing a violent tremor to shake the framework of the building.

Katz immediately slammed a boot into the front door, kicking it open. The Israeli charged inside, his Uzi held ready. The Phoenix Force commander scrambled to a stack of crates for cover, and held his fire. None of the enemy appeared to offer an immediate threat.

Several stevedores lay senseless on the floor. Others clasped their hands over their ears. Only two or three thugs had weapons in hand. None had apparently noticed Katzenelenbogen.

Gary Manning bolted around the corner to the rear of the warehouse. He virtually ran into two goons. One stevedore was down on one knee, head cradled between his hands. The other hood held an old M-14 assault rifle in his fists. The guy swung his weapon at Manning, but the Canadian stepped forward and parried the rifle with the barrel of his shotgun.

The enemy gunman triggered his M-14. A bullet screamed past Manning's right shoulder, close enough to send shards of ice up the Phoenix fighter's spine. Manning's Remington roared. A burst of buckshot smashed into the thug's face and literally ripped his head off.

The stevedore who knelt on the plank walk recoiled from his comrade's decapitated corpse when it fell beside him, blood gushing from the ragged stump of its neck. Horrified, the stevedore tried to rise. Manning rapidly closed in and hammered the bottom of his fist into the nerve junction between the guy's neck and shoulder. The blow doubled him up to receive Manning's knee to the face. The man fell to the plank walk in an unconscious heap.

Manning worked the pump to feed a fresh shell to the hungry breech. The Canadian pivoted as he jacked the round home and discovered another gun-wielding hoodlum had stepped from the back door of the building. Manning fired the Remington. A swarm of Number Four pellets plowed into the gunman's chest and hurled him back into the warehouse.

A figure moved at the corner of the building. Manning pumped the Remington's action and swung the shotgun toward the movement. David McCarter held up his left palm to urge Manning to hold his fire. The Canadian nodded as he lowered his shotgun.

Suddenly McCarter lunged forward and aimed his Ingram machine pistol at a trio of enemy gunmen who charged across the pier from the gangplank of *Le Monarque*. The Briton's M-10 spat a 3-round burst that nailed the closest attacker in the chest. The impact of 9mm slugs sent the gunman's body tumbling across the plank walk. McCarter squeezed off another quick salvo that ripped a diagonal line in an opponent's torso from rib cage to breastbone.

The second hoodlum fell, but the third gunman dived to the planks as a volley of parabellum bullets burned air above his prone form. The thug pointed a Walther P-38 at McCarter. The battle-wise Briton ducked back to the edge of the building before the gunman could pull the trigger. However, McCarter would have been safe, anyway. Manning's shotgun bellowed, and buckshot pulverized the hood's skull. The Walther slipped, unfired, from the dead man's fingers.

Another pair of enemy gunmen had rushed to the aid

of their comrades. When they saw Manning and McCarter cut down their buddies in a matter of seconds, the two buttonmen bolted to the cover of a pile of wooden crates. McCarter took an M-26 frag grenade from his belt, pulled the pin and tossed the minibomb at the hoods' position. The grenade hit the pier and rolled behind the crates. One of the thugs reached for the M-26, hoping to throw it back at McCarter.

The grenade exploded in his face.

Splintered wood, chunks of cheap pottery and fragments of two dismembered bodies were scattered all over the pier. Another grenade sailed over the roof of the warehouse and landed on the plank walk. Billows of dark smoke rose from the sputtering canister, creating a thick green cloud across Hermit Harbor. McCarter and Manning recognized the signal. They quickly unsnapped the canvas cases that hung on each commando's left hip. The two Phoenix Force warriors removed their M-17 gas masks and hastily pulled the contraptions over their heads.

"Glad to see Alby and his blokes haven't gone to sleep," McCarter commented, his voice muffled by the filters of the mask.

"Better see if Katz needs any help and—" Manning ended his sentence abruptly when he saw the activity aboard the ship.

Several Corsicans and stevedores had set up a mounted machine gun on the deck of *La Monarque*. The weapon was pointed at McCarter and Manning as the enemy opened fire.

15

Colonel Katzenelenbogen did not need any help.

The Israeli commando crouched as he moved behind the columns of crates inside the warehouse. The enemy forces inside the building were still dazed and confused and unaware of Katz's presence. Many of the hoodlums were still sprawled unconscious on the floor. None of the flunkies had escaped unscathed. Every crooked stevedore had suffered at least one ruptured eardrum or bleeding nostrils from the double blast of concussion grenades.

Three stevedores had already bolted out the back door to find Manning and McCarter waiting for them. Katz counted four thugs still on their feet. Only one man noticed the front door was open. The guy slowly approached, a .45-caliber Star PD in his fist. Katz crouched by the edge of a crate and waited for the gun-man to draw closer.

The Israeli's prosthesis lashed out, chopping the steel hooks across the stevedore's wrist. The blow knocked the pistol from the hoodlum's hand. Katz quickly jammed the three-prong hook under the startled goon's jaw and clamped the metal talons around his opponent's throat.

Katz flexed muscles in his right arm to increase the pressure of the hooked grip. The steel blades pierced flesh. Blood jetted from a severed artery as the man convulsed like a fish at the end of a line. Katz held the Uzi in his left fist and braced the metal stock against his hip. He aimed at the trio of horrified hoodlums at the opposite end of the warehouse and squeezed the trigger.

A salvo of parabellum rounds plastered a stevedore against a wall, crimson oozing from his bullet-ravaged chest. Katz shifted the aim of his Uzi and hosed another goon with 9mm death. The guy's body hit the floor and skidded across the sawdust-covered surface like a bloodied bobsled. However, the last gunman managed to dive behind a wall of crates before the Phoenix Force commander could burn him with copper-jacketed brimstone.

Katz opened the steel talons at the end of his right arm to release his first opponent. The man's corpse sunk to the floor, his throat crushed into gory pulp. The Israeli retreated to the cover of the crates as a shotgun boomed from the other end of the column. Buckshot chewed at the rim of a wooden box less than a foot from Katz's position.

The Israeli yanked open the canvas case on his right hip and removed an M-17 gas mask. He was confident the remaining gunman would not venture out from shelter for a minute or two, long enough for Katz to slip the protective mask over his face. The Phoenix Force pro knew that Major Alby's team would be arriving soon and they had been instructed to fire tear-gas grenades before they closed in.

Katz did not have to wait very long. A canister shattered a windowpane and landed inside the warehouse. The grenade slid across the floor to the center of the room, spewing CS tear gas. Protected by the M-16, Katz waited for the gas to affect the hidden gunman who lurked at the opposite end of the crates.

The man stumbled into view, coughing and choking as the tear gas filled his lungs and throat. Half-blind, the stevedore still pumped another shell into the breech of his Winchester riot gun and tried to aim it at Katz's position. The Israeli warrior had no choice. He blasted a trio of 9mm slugs into his opponent's chest. The hood dropped his scattergun and fell back against a corner of a crate.

Katz advanced slowly, glancing from body to body in case any of the enemy were playing possum. Three figures entered the building. The Israeli turned but raised his Uzi when he saw the trio also wore gas masks. The bulky black figure of Major Alby greeted the Phoenix commander with a wave as he kept his 9mm Sterling sub-machine gun pointed at the floor.

"Good Lord," Alby remarked. "You chaps didn't leave us much to do, did you?"

"Check these bodies carefully," Katz instructed. "Don't take any chances with the wounded. A wounded man can still be dangerous. Cuff them and frisk them carefully."

"All right," the major replied.

Katz noticed the other two SIS agents carried M-79 grenade launchers as well as Sterling subguns. The Israeli pointed his prosthesis at one of the launchers.

"Is that thing loaded?" he asked.

"Yes, sir," the agent replied.

"Let me have it," Katz ordered as he slipped the sling of the Uzi onto his shoulder. "And an extra tear-gas grenade."

"What are you going to do?" Alby asked with a frown.

"Join the rest of my team," the Israeli answered simply.

THE CORSICAN SYNDICATE GOONS on board *Le Monarque* had set up a French Model 52 light machine gun mounted on an M-2 tripod. They opened fire on the pier, raking the storagehouse with 7.5mm projectiles. Gary Manning and David McCarter had barely managed to dive to the plank walk in time to avoid being cut in halves by the murderous stream of full-auto hell.

The Phoenix Force pair were surprised when the machine gun sprayed a continuous volley across the area, bullets punching into the warehouse, away from their position. Manning glanced up and peered through the dense green fog created by the smoke canister. He could see little except the outline of the ship and the orange flame of the M-52 muzzle-flash.

"They aren't concentrating fire on us," the Canadian declared. "Must be blinded by the smoke. The machine gunners are hosing the pier, trying to pin us down."

"I think they're succeeding," McCarter replied, wiping a lens of his M-17 mask. "And when the wind blows the smoke away from our position, those bastards will be able to pick us off."

"Christ," Manning muttered. "Where the hell is the rest of the assault team? Did they lose their way to Hermit Harbor?"

"Don't worry," the Briton chuckled. "If we get killed in action, Brognola will see to it we get a nice funeral."

Just then, two figures emerged from the water at the starboard quarter of *Le Monarque*. Calvin James and Rafael Encizo found handholds by the transom gate.

They pulled off their diving flippers to climb barefoot, toes gripping the slippery surface. Encizo's left hand clawed the gunwale until he could pull himself higher to hook the butt of his speargun over the handrail.

The Cuban glanced around the deck of the enemy vessel. Satisfied that none of the opposition was aft, Encizo hauled himself over the rail. He reached over the side and caught James's hand to help the black commando climb to the top.

Both men quickly unbuckled their Emerson diving tanks and face masks. The sound of the enemy's M-52 machine gun urged the pair to act quickly. Encizo held his speargun ready and watched for unfriendly forces while James drew a Marine Combat Bowie from an ankle sheath and slit the seal to his waterproof bag.

A Corsican sailor, armed with a MAT-49 submachine gun, suddenly appeared from the companionway at the port deck. The gunman spied the two Phoenix Force invaders dressed in black wetsuits. He rapidly worked the bolt of his MAT to chamber a 9mm cartridge. Encizo snap-aimed his speargun and pulled the trigger.

A two-foot-long missile sliced through the night and slammed into the Corsican's chest. The steel tip pierced the man's heart. The gunman tumbled back across the threshold of the companionway and fell from view.

"Things are gonna get real hot real soon," the Cuban announced as he lowered his empty speargun.

"Yeah," James agreed, taking his M-76 submachine gun from the bag. "That's why we're here."

Another Corsican buttonman jogged toward the starboard, a 9mm MAB pistol in his fist. James had unfolded the wire stock of his Smith & Wesson chopper and shoved a magazine into the well, but he had not chambered a round yet. However, Encizo's hand flashed to the leather pouch on his hip and quickly drew out a star-shaped *shaken*.

The Cuban's arm lashed out and released the six-pointed throwing star. The *shaken* whirled toward the Corsican gunman and struck the thug's face, a steel tine puncturing his left eyeball. He screamed as the MAB autoloader fell from his trembling fingers. The Corsican touched the star buried in his eye socket before he collapsed in a lifeless glob on the deck.

"Thanks, Keio," Encizo whispered. The late Keio Ohara, one of the original five men of Phoenix Force, had instructed the Cuban in *shuriken-jutsu*. Encizo's skill in this martial art had saved his life more than once.

"Okay, man," James declared as he screwed a foot-long sound suppressor to the threaded muzzle of his M-76. "Get your goodies."

The Cuban sliced open his waterproof bag while James stood guard. Excited voices cried out from the companionway. More Corsican thugs had discovered their slain comrade with the spear in his chest. Two syndicate goons cautiously crossed the threshold, the barrels of their MAT subguns moving to and fro like insect antennae.

Calvin James aimed his M-76 and opened fire. The silenced chatterbox popped like a series of exploding firecrackers. Parabellum bullets slashed into the enemy gunmen, blasting the life out of the Corsican flunkies.

Another adversary appeared at the handrail of the fly bridge. The gangster held a 5.56mm FAMAS automatic rifle. The Corsican syndicate had stolen two hundred of these compact, bullpup-style weapons from the French arsenal at Saint-Étienne. The syndicate had sold half the guns to the French Red Brigade terrorists and kept the rest for their own use. The gunman on the bridge leaned forward and aimed his FAMAS at Calvin James.

The hood was too slow. James suddenly raised his M-76 and fired a rapid volley. Nine-millimeter slugs tore into the Corsican's solar plexus, breastbone and throat. The gunman shrieked as he staggered along the length of the handrail and triggered his FAMAS, a final act of desperation seconds before he died. The French music box chattered a loud funeral dirge, pumping half a dozen rounds into Lucaya Bay.

Rafael Encizo took an M-26 grenade from his water-proof bag, yanked out the pin and hurled it through the open hatch of the companionway. James followed his example and threw in a second grenade. The twin explosions sent a violent shiver through the ship. Glass burst from portholes along the side of the ship.

"Merde, alors!" a voice cried out as black smoke rose from the burning diesel engine below deck.

"This is the Coastal Patrol!" an amplified voice announced from a bullhorn as two speedboats rapidly approached the starboard of *Le Monarque*. "Throw down your weapons and—"

Several Corsican killers opened fire on the closest patrol boat, blocking out the bullhorn. Bullets kicked geysers of water all around the smaller vessel. Holes appeared in the port side of the boat. Windows to the sliding doors of the cabin shattered, and the pilot threw up his hands as two slugs buried themselves in his spine.

The patrol boat swung out of control and rocketed bow first into the wooden supports of the pier. Fiberglass crushed against the thick pillars. The Corsicans continued to blast the crippled craft with a deadly rain of bullets. Sparks ignited a leaky fuel tank, and the explosion tore the patrol boat apart and sent flaming debris hurtling across the bay.

The gangsters did not get to celebrate their victory. Calvin James lobbed a grenade at the group of killers in charge of the M-52 machine gun. The fragmentation explosive transformed men and machine into bloodied chunks of raw meat and twisted metal. With the machine gun out of operation, the remaining three men of Phoenix Force were able to attack the enemy vessel.

Yakov Katzenelenbogen aimed the M-79 grenade launcher and squeezed the trigger. The weapon resembles a sawed-off shotgun with an enormous bore, and the recoil of the M-79 buttstock against Katz's hip was similar to that of a 10-gauge shotgun. Yet no buckshot pattern or deerslayer slug could match the destructive capabilities of a 40mm grenade.

The shell Katz fired was a CS tear-gas canister, and the explosion released a thick cloud of pungent gas across the bow of *Le Monarque*. The Israeli broke open the M-79, removed the spent cartridge casing and shoved a second CS grenade into the breech. He aimed carefully and lobbed the explosive into the fly bridge, breaking a window in one of the top cabins. Katz discarded the grenade launcher and unslung his Uzi.

McCarter and Manning charged up the gangplank, weapons held ready. Two gun-wielding stevedores had fled behind the great bronze elephant statue for cover. McCarter noticed their legs when he glanced under the metal beast's belly. The Briton dropped to one knee and fired his M-10 Ingram, blasting a treacherous volley under the elephant. Parabellum rounds smashed into the stevedores' legs, shattering shin bones as if they were toothpicks. The hoodlums screamed and collapsed to the deck. McCarter triggered his machine pistol again and silenced the pair forever.

Manning saw another stevedore duck behind the rear of a forklift. The guy pawed at his tear-filled eyes, trying to clear his vision to use the Argentine Sistema Colt pistol. Manning's Remington roared, and a burst of buckshot slammed into the guy's exposed left arm and shoulder. The results were not pretty. Number Four pellets slashed the limb into a mangled shred of flesh and muscle draped over shattered bone. The hapless stevedore dropped his weapon and passed out from the tremendous shock of the horrific injury.

Suddenly another stevedore charged from the front of the forklift. He closed in fast, swinging a crate hook at Manning's broad back. The Canadian whirled and raised his shotgun to block the attack. The steel hook snared the frame of Manning's Remington, and the brawny longshoreman adroitly yanked the riot gun from the Phoenix fighter's grasp.

The stevedore raised his hook again, prepared to bury the metal tip in Manning's skull. The Canadian stepped forward and slammed the heel of his left hand into the guy's forearm before he could swing the hook. Manning's right fist jabbed a short hard punch to his opponent's mouth.

Manning seized the stevedore's arm with both hands and pivoted to drive his hip into the guy's groin. The Canadian braced the thug's arm across his shoulder, locking the elbow. Then he yanked down hard. Bone cracked and the stevedore screamed. The hook dropped to the deck at Manning's feet.

The Canadian turned and spun his opponent around. He grabbed him from behind, seizing the man's collar and belt. Manning ran to the nearest handrail and flung the stevedore over the top. The guy shouted an obscenity as he plunged headfirst into Lucaya Bay.

Raul Ortega and his two personal bodyguards, Luis Gonzales and Ricardo Martinez, ran along the starboard side of *Le Monarque*. The Colombian syndicate kingpin and his enforcers had been sent to supervise the arrival of the heroin shipment from France. All had gone well. The ship arrived an hour ahead of schedule, there was no evidence the police suspected anything and the security of the operation had seemed airtight.

Then all hell broke loose, coming from every direction at once. *¡Madre de Dios!* Explosions were going off all over the ship. People were shooting from everywhere, and now the air was thick with tear gas. The Corsicans were supposed to be tough and they were armed with high-quality military weapons, but whoever had masterminded the assault was a lot tougher and far more professional than the gangsters were.

Fuck the heroin and fuck MERGE. Ortega would worry about Don Fazzio and the others later. All that mattered at the moment was getting off *La Monarque* alive. Ortega had drawn a compact .380 Astra Constable, but he did not intend to use his pistol. That was the sort of work Gonzales and Martinez were paid to handle.

Ortega was sandwiched between his bodyguards. Gonzales carried a Brazilian 9mm Uru submachine gun and Martinez held a .45-caliber Llama autoloader in his big hairy fist. The enforcers were the best soldiers on Ortega's payroll. He only hoped they were good enough to help him fight his way off the damn ship.

Suddenly a figure dressed in shiny black rubber appeared in their path. Rafael Encizo had donned an M-17 gas mask when the first trace of CS assaulted his nostrils. The bug-eyed lenses and hog-snout filter looked bizarre with the wetsuit. Encizo could have been a humanoid sea monster or a creature from outer space. Indeed, his Heckler & Koch MP-5 machine pistol was as menacing as any space-age laser gun.

Gonzales, half-blind from tear gas and a bit slow mentally under the best conditions, was no match for the Cuban war machine. Encizo raised and fired his H&K blaster before the Colombian goon fully realized the figure in black was more than just a shadow. A trio of 9mm missiles split Gonzales's face and rearranged his brains. Ortega screamed in fear and revulsion when a spray of blood and gray matter splattered his face.

Martinez hurried past his boss and quickly shoved Gonzales's corpse, using his slain partner as a combination shield and battering ram. The dead man collided with Encizo, driving him into the handrail. The Cuban's forearm struck hard and his fingers opened, dropping his MP-5 over the side. The machine pistol splashed as it broke the surface to sink into the depths of the bay.

But the loss of the H&K did not make Rafael Encizo a helpless target. He quickly gripped the handrail for leverage and thrust a bare foot into Gonzales's corpse, kicking it back at Martinez. The dead man fell against the Colombian triggerman. Martinez grunted and pushed the corpse out of his way as he tried to aim his Llama pistol at Encizo.

The Phoenix Force veteran had not retreated. He had drawn from an ankle sheath a Cold Steel Tanto, six inches of steel blade with an ultrasharp edge and a reinforced point. The rubberized handle assures a firm grip. Encizo had studied *tanto-jutsu* under Keio Ohara and continued to develop his skill at the Japanese knife-fighting martial art since Ohara's death.

Encizo slashed Martinez's wrist before the Colombian could adjust the aim of his pistol. The heavy blade chopped through flesh and muscle and cut to the bone. Martinez shrieked in agony as his Llama fell from useless fingers. Encizo drove the point of the Tanto into his opponent's solar plexus and pulled the blade up to the sternal notch. Blood poured across the Cuban's wrist as Martinez convulsed in a final spasm of death.

Raul Ortega lost his nerve. The Colombian bolted toward the bow when he realized his bodyguards were as good as dead. Encizo left the Tanto buried in Martinez's chest and instantly reached for the pouch on his hip. The Cuban drew a *shaken* star and hurled it at the fleeing Colombian.

The multipointed projectile chased Ortega and smacked into him between the shoulder blades. The Colombian's mouth opened in a silent scream when the sharp steel pierced his spine. Ortega stumbled several feet, the *shaken* lodged in his back like a metallic tumor. Then the Colombian fell on his belly near the bronze elephant.

The fire below deck had spread to a storage compartment where diving gear was kept. The flames ignited four tanks containing oxygen. A fierce explosion shook *Le Monarque*. The vibrations rocked the ship so violently that the elephant statue tipped over.

It crashed down on Raul Ortega, crushing the Colombian like a cockroach.

The battle was over. Only a handful of Corsicans and crooked stevedores survived the assault. They surrendered to the five-man army known as Phoenix Force.

Alby and his agents mounted the gangplank as two Coastal Patrol boats pulled up to the pier.

"Round up these lice," Colonel Katzenelenbogen instructed. "We'll figure out what to do with them later."

"What happened here?" Major Alby inquired as he gazed down at Ortega's arm jutting from beneath the elephant.

"Just a fella who bit off more than he could chew," Encizo replied with a shrug. "Everything sort of piled up on him, I guess."

16

"This is all I have been able to find on the island of Stella," Major Alby announced as he handed Katz a file.

Alby and the men of Phoenix Force met at the secret base at the warehouse near Nassau the morning after the assault on Hermit Harbor. Although three members of the Coastal Patrol had been killed during the battle, there was no doubt that Phoenix Force and the Bahamian authorities had won. It had been the biggest blow dealt to MERGE thus far, but the mission was not over yet.

Paul Wainwright had talked his figurative head off. To cross-check Wainwright's claims, Calvin James had interrogated him under the influence of scopolamine, as well. The informer told them the same story. The Bahamian headquarters of MERGE was located on Stella Island.

"The island is one of almost seven hundred tiny land masses in the Bahamas," Alby explained, leafing through his copy of the file folder. "As Wainwright stated, Stella is located in the Exuma Sound, approximately ninety-five miles from the coast of San Salvador. It was purchased in 1983 by a man calling himself Mario Contare. Apparently this is actually Don Fazzio, although that, too, may be a phony name."

"Any idea how many people are staying on that island?" Rafael Encizo inquired.

"Contare—or Fazzio—has a security force living on the island," Alby answered. "Officially this consists of twenty-five men. All are from the United States, and they have special government permits to own and carry full-auto weapons while patrolling Stella Island. It is very likely that there are thirty or more men stationed at the island. In the Bahamas, we get a lot of rich eccentric chaps who come here for privacy. Frankly no one really wants to bother wealthy landowners who pay a great deal of taxes."

"Capitalism can't function without capital," Gary Manning said with a shrug. "How big is Stella Island?"

"Less than ten square miles," the major replied. "And that's including a lot of coral reef that isn't much use to anyone except the crabs and sea gulls. All the buildings and such are located inland."

"What kind of power systems does the island have?" Rafael Encizo inquired.

"Apparently the island has turbogenerators powered by ocean water," Alby said. "But they've also got a solar unit on the island, and I would assume they also have an emergency setup of diesel generators, as well. Totally self-sufficient. No problem with fresh water, either, owing to a series of underground rivers. Fazzio spends a fortune on food and wine and such that is flown out to Stella from New Providence or San Salvador."

"Sounds like a real hardsite," Calvin James mused. "We might be able to cut off supplies, but we don't have time to wait for them to starve."

"We don't have time, period," Katz declared as he

fired a Camel cigarette. "Fazzio and the other members of MERGE have their own intelligence network in the Bahamas. By now they probably know about Hermit Harbor. They know that their people in the stevedore union have either been arrested or killed, and they probably assume we squeezed information out of Wainwright."

"They're professionals," McCarter agreed. "But even professionals make mistakes. Letting Wainwright into the fold was a mistake. He's not the sort to keep his mouth shut under pressure. Bloody lucky for us."

"Sure," the Israeli agreed, "MERGE has made mistakes, but don't count on them making many more. They haven't established an international criminal network by being careless. Within twenty-four hours, Fazzio and his people will flee Stella Island and the Bahamas."

"Yeah," Manning said grimly. "And it's anybody's guess where they'll go. The United States, South America, Europe, anywhere."

"That means we have to move fast," Encizo stated.

"Wait a minute," Major Alby began. "I can't assemble a fleet of armed men to accompany you on this assault. You saw what happened last night. I managed to get a few SIS agents, a handful of customs officers and three patrol boats—and none of them was worth a damn in a combat situation. Besides, authorizing a raid on a group of heroin smugglers is one thing, but launching a full-scale attack on a privately owned island that belongs to a man who frequently plays golf with certain judges and members of parliament is quite another. Fazzio might be a Mafia don, but Mario Contare is a respected member of several elite country clubs in New

Providence and San Salvador. According to his file, Contare occasionally visits Freeport, where he is also very welcome. He's a member of the Underwater Explorers' Society and every year he gives UNEXSO a nice large contribution.''

"Major," Katz said as he crushed out his cigarette in a scallop-shaped ashtray, "we can't let Fazzio get away."

"But you five can't take on the entire island by yourselves," Alby insisted. "The information I've given you certainly isn't enough."

"Added to what Wainwright has told us about the island," James commented, "it'll have to do."

"Maybe not," McCarter declared. "We'll have to move our base to San Salvador, anyway, mates. Why not a quick air recon of the island of Stella while we're at it?"

"I've got a C-130 ready for transport," Alby said. "A bit large for recon."

"What about lending me another chopper?" the Briton inquired. "Don't need a pilot. If it flies, I can handle it."

"I can probably get you a Bell HH-K1 on short notice," the major replied. "But it won't be armed."

"It'll have to do," McCarter said with a shrug. "Besides, I don't want to tangle with the bastards with a hit-and-run from the air. Just plan to get a better look at their setup to help us launch an all-out strike."

"Good idea, Mr. Daniels," Katz agreed. "Who wants to accompany him on the recon?"

"I can't say I really *want* to," Manning sighed. "But I will. So long as Mr. Daniels promises not to play daredevil when he gets in his flying machine."

"Heaven forbid," McCarter replied with a wiry grin.

"Shit," Manning muttered.

COLUMBUS DAY is still celebrated in the United States on October 8, although Columbus did not reach the shores of what is now the United States of America.

In fact, Columbus "discovered" one of the eastern islands of the Bahamas. Most historians believe this island was probably San Salvador. The residents of the island certainly agree. In fact, there are numerous markers found at different points on San Salvador that claim to be the exact spot where Columbus and his crew first set foot in the New World.

David McCarter piloted the Bell helicopter over Watling Castle at the southwestern tip of San Salvador. George Watling was a legendary pirate. In fact, until 1926 the island that is now San Salvador had been called Watling Island.

Gary Manning gazed down at the ruins of the old castle. The Canadian thought it ironic to pass over the remnants of a pirate of the past in quest of a pirate fortress of the present. Manning wondered if anything ever really changes.

The HH-K1 chopper hovered over the blue-green surface of the Atlantic and moved northwest to the Exuma Sound. McCarter and Manning found a number of small islands in the area, but they had no trouble identifying Stella Island.

A rim of dark coral surrounded the shores of the tiny land mass. Three buildings were located at the center of the island. The largest structure was a modern split-level house with a Spanish-style tile roof. Manning examined the roof with the aid of a pair of Minolta 10x40 binoculars and noticed several rectangular panels.

"Photovoltaic cells," he announced, shouting to be heard above the roar of the rotor blades. "Used for solar energy."

"Maybe we should hope for an eclipse," McCarter said as he worked cyclic and collective controls to maintain a hover.

Manning continued to scan the island through his binoculars. The house featured two large picture windows that seemed to reflect very little light. The Canadian guessed the glass was probably bullet resistant. He trained the field glasses on another building, a long single-story structure made of wood with a shingle roof. A young man sat on the porch steps, smoking a cigarette as he leafed through a skin magazine. A Thompson submachine gun was propped against the handrail.

"Looks like billets down there," Manning told McCarter. "A guy's goofing off on guard duty. Guess you just can't get good help these days."

"I'm going to fly around to the other side of the island," McCarter declared, gradually applying pressure to the rudders.

The Bell chopper swung in an arch around the island of Stella. McCarter moved the helicopter a bit closer and eased back the cyclic to reduce speed. Manning peered through his Minolta spyglass as the whirlybird made its pass.

At the rear of the house was a patio and a large kidney-shaped pool. Three men lounged in wicker lawn chairs, sipping iced tea as they conversed. The discussion ended abruptly as they heard the thunder of the helicopter blades. The trio turned their heads to gaze up at the Bell HH-K1.

"Well," Manning said, "they know we're here."

"We'll be gone before they can do anything about it," McCarter assured him. "What do you make of that fence?"

The Briton referred to a fifteen-foot-high steel link fence that surrounded the estate. Manning scanned the barrier and finally located a sign that warned of danger and high voltage.

"It's electrified," Manning announced. "These guys don't want to make it easy for us."

"Bloody inconsiderate," the Briton muttered.

McCarter piloted the Bell chopper over a large parade field. Manning got a good look at the third building. It was actually three structures connected together. Hangars for the trio of Sikorsky HSS-2 helicopters that stood on a flight pad nearby.

"Holy shit," Manning growled. "Where the hell did they get those choppers from?"

"I don't think we'd better land and ask them," the Briton replied. "What's that over by the shore? The part that isn't covered with coral."

Manning examined the flimsy tentlike structure that appeared to be a huge canvas draped over a wooden frame. The Canadian saw the tip of the bow of a small boat at the corner of the lean-to.

"I think it's a shelter for small vessels," Manning answered. "Probably speedboats."

"There's a lot of movement going on down there," McCarter commented, glancing down at the figures darting from the billets and the main house. Most carried weapons. "If any of those blokes have a high-powered rifle with a telescopic sight, we could be in trouble, mate.''

"I think we've seen all we're going to see this trip," the Canadian declared. "Let's head back to our new base and...."

Manning saw something move at the flight pad. He turned his binoculars toward the Sikorsky choppers below. The rotor blades of two aircraft had begun to spin. One helicopter rose into the air. The muzzles of two machine guns jutted from under the Sikorsky's nose.

17

David McCarter turned the throttle to increase speed as the Sikorsky ascended. The British flying ace steered the Bell HH-K1 for San Salvador, while Manning reached for a canvas pack at his feet. The enemy helicopter followed the Phoenix Force craft, but held its fire until it could get within effective range.

"What have you got in your bag of tricks, Gary?" McCarter asked, moving the cyclic control forward.

"Plastic explosives," the Canadian demolitions expert answered. "Some C-4 and some C-3 I got from Alby. Also some CV-38, but I don't see what use that'll be under the circumstances."

"I thought you might have a grenade launcher tucked away in there," McCarter commented. "Too bad we didn't pack some heat-seeking missiles or a .50-caliber machine gun."

"This was suppose to be just a recon mission," Manning stated as he pushed a glob of C-4 into a round cardboard tube. "But I guess the enemy doesn't like us playing peekaboo."

"Fuck 'em if they can't take a joke," the Briton growled.

The Sikorsky was closing in fast, its .50-caliber guns spitting a stream of destruction. Most of the big projectiles fell short of the target, but two or three slugs smashed into the tail of the Bell chopper. The impact rocked the Phoenix copter. McCarter struggled with the controls to stay on course.

"Can you get us higher?" Manning asked, inserting a pencil detonator into the explosives inside the tube. "We need to get above the other chopper."

"I think I know what you've got in mind," McCarter remarked. "If it doesn't work, we'll be scattered all over the Atlantic."

"Since when did you worry about a little risk, David?" the Canadian inquired.

"Just wanted to make sure you knew what the stakes are, mate."

"If you've got a better idea," Manning began.

"Hang on," McCarter announced sharply. "We're going up as fast as I can get this bird to go."

The Briton applied pressure to the cyclic and turned the Bell to the right, westward into the wind. He then raised the collective in a single smooth motion and opened the throttle. The HH-K1 rose swiftly and climbed high above the pursuing Sikorsky.

The enemy craft failed to follow McCarter's abrupt maneuver. The Sikorsky pilot's reflexes lacked the Briton's battle-honed edge. He triggered a volley of machine-gun fire, blasting twin columns of .50-caliber rounds at the sky. Suddenly the Bell chopper seemed to disappear. Too late, the Sikorsky pilot realized his quarry was now directly overhead.

Gary Manning set the timer of the pencil detonator and opened the sliding door of the Bell. He dropped the cardboard tube outside. The lightweight projectile fell toward the Sikorsky as McCarter thrust the throttle forward. The Bell shot away from the enemy chopper as the tube danced briefly above the rotor blades of the Sikorsky, caught in a powerful air current from the force of the blades.

The tube began to fly away from the enemy craft. Then it exploded. A quarter pound of C-4 erupted, blasting the rotor and carriage of the Sikorsky. The Plexiglas windows were blown apart. The great rotor blades ripped from the metal head. The blast ignited the fuel tank, and the Sikorsky exploded into a ball of flame. Mangled metal wreckage plunged to the sea below.

Shock waves from the explosions swung the Bell off course. McCarter allowed the chopper to ride with the motion before he worked the controls to get back on course. The Briton sighed with relief and gave his partner a thumbs-up salute. Manning nodded and returned the gesture.

The two Phoenix Force commandos were glad to see the shore of San Salvador in the distance. McCarter steered the helicopter along the coast, searching for the new Phoenix base located on the outskirts of Cockburn Town.

"What the hell was that?" Manning asked with alarm when he heard a metallic ring from somewhere in the undercarriage of the chopper.

Another sour tune erupted, accompanied by the whine of a projectile against metal. Manning and McCarter scanned the waters below and found the source of their new problem. Two men in a speedboat were cutting through the waves. One man steered the vessel while his companion worked the bolt to a long-barreled rifle with a telescopic sight mounted to its frame.

"These bastards are really pissed with us," Manning muttered as he rigged another C-4 tube bomb.

"Bloke must be having trouble trying to hit a moving object from a speeding boat," McCarter commented. "I'll try to make it a little more difficult for the bugger."

The Briton applied forceful pressure on the cyclic to execute a steep, sharp turn. As the copter started the maneuver, McCarter used the collective to maintain altitude and the throttle to increase speed. He repeated the maneuver, turning the cyclic to the opposite direction to form a zigzag pattern. The enemy rifleman shifted the aim of his weapon back and forth, trying to follow the movement of the Bell HH-K1. Frustrated, he fired his rifle and completely missed the bird.

"Ready!" Manning announced as he inserted a pencil detonator into the C-4.

"Set the bloody timer," McCarter told him. "I'm takin' us around now."

The chopper swung a wide circle and headed back toward the boat. The pilot of the vessel brought it to a full halt while the rifleman stood up and placed the stock of his weapon to a shoulder. The sniper aimed carefully; the cross hairs of his telescope sights centered on David McCarter's chest. Kill the pilot, kill the chopper.

However, McCarter suddenly raised the collective and worked the throttle to elevate the Bell aircraft. The sniper squeezed the trigger. A .300 Winchester Magnum tore into the underbelly of the HH-K1. Manning and McCarter heard the bullet strike, felt the impact ride through the hull of their craft.

Manning shoved open his door and hurled the improvised bomb at the enemy boat below. The tube landed dead center in the middle of the vessel. It detonated less than a second after it hit. The explosion shattered the boat as if it were a fragile sculpture made of thin ice.

There wasn't enough left of the two hoodlums to bury them in a thimble.

"That's that," Manning announced, wiping the back of a hand across his sweaty brow.

Without warning, a salvo of high-velocity bullets ripped into the tail pylon of the Bell. The slugs smashed the tail rotor and the horizontal stabilizer. The chopper spun into a wild pivoting motion. As the craft spun about, McCarter and Manning saw their assailant.

Another Sikorsky helicopter had appeared out of nowhere and caught the Phoenix Force chopper off guard.

"We can't stay up," McCarter declared, gripping the collective and cyclic controls. "Brace yourself, mate. We're not going to land easy."

He lowered the collective and pulled back the cyclic as he increased pressure on the rudders. The Bell descended awkwardly, still spinning out of control. The enemy copter fired another volley of .50-caliber missiles. Bullets ripped through the metal skin and drilled into the machinery of the Bell HH-K1. McCarter and Manning smelled petrol from a ruptured gas line.

The Briton shifted aft pressure to the cyclic and pushed down on the collective. McCarter realized that a crash landing might spark metal and ignite the fuel leak, but there was no other option. The bird came down hard, the skids striking the sandy surface of a beach.

The Phoenix Force pair were jarred by the rough landing, but neither man was harmed and the fuel tank did not catch fire. However, the Sikorsky still hovered like a harpy, ready to finish off McCarter and Manning.

The enemy aircraft might have blasted the Bell HH-K1 and the two Phoenix warriors to oblivion if the Sikorsky pilot had not mistakenly believed the Bell chopper was already history. The enemy helicopter had swung off from the bullet-ravaged HH-K1, circling away to be clear of the explosion that seemed certain when the crippled craft crash-landed.

The Sikorsky quickly completed the circle and tried to move into position to destroy the Bell with another burst of .50-caliber blitzers. McCarter and Manning leaped from the wrecked Bell copter, weapons in hand. The pair dashed for the cover of a cluster of boulders above the beach as the Sikorsky opened fire once more.

A salvo of machine-gun slugs peppered the immobile HH-K1. The ruptured fuel line caught sparks, and flame rode to the tanks. The Bell exploded. Mangled steel was blasted into the sky and across the beach.

The Phoenix Force pair had already reached the cover of the boulders. Manning carried his canvas pack of explosives and the Remington shotgun. McCarter had his trusted M-10 Ingram and Browning Hi-Power automatic in shoulder leather. These weapons seemed puny compared to the .50-caliber guns of the enemy Sikorsky.

The helicopter hovered forward, machine guns blazing. Heavy bullets slammed into boulders, cracking and chipping stone. McCarter and Manning stayed low. The shadow of the Sikorsky fell across them as the enemy craft passed over their position.

The Sikorsky needed to shift position in order to lower its nose to fire down on the Phoenix Force pair. When it completed the pass, McCarter and Manning rose up and opened fire on the great mechanical vulture. The Briton blasted a volley of 9mm rounds into the Plexiglas window by the pilot's seat while Manning pumped a burst of shotgun pellets at the tail of the Sikorsky.

The enemy chopper bolted away from the boulders, the pilot trying to operate the controls with one hand while he pawed at the bullet-torn flesh and splintered bone that had been his left arm. The buckshot blast had ruined the tail rotor and horizontal stabilizer. The Sikorsky spun and whirled, just as the Bell HH-K1 had before.

And like the Bell, the Sikorsky crash-landed to the beach, nose first. The windscreen collapsed. Metal crunched on impact. Nothing alive would be taken from the wrecked helicopter.

"Well," McCarter said with a grin, "I'd say our little recon mission turned out pretty well."

"You would," Manning replied sourly.

MAJ. PENDEXTER ALBY was astonished by the report Manning and McCarter delivered. However, the other members of Phoenix Force were neither surprised by how their colleagues had handled their pursuers or alarmed by the information about Stella Island.

"There is no way the five of you can attack that place by yourselves," Alby remarked. "But I think I can get some troops after I explain about that helicopter chase, which is pretty solid evidence that all the other claims about Stella Island are true."

"That would take too long," Katzenelenbogen replied. "If Fazzio and the other members of MERGE weren't already planning to pull out, they'll waste no time when those two choppers and that speedboat don't return."

"Sorry," McCarter said with a shrug. "Blokes didn't give us much choice."

"Oh, I'm not criticizing how you two handled the situation," Katz assured him. "In fact, the enemies' transportation capabilities have certainly been impaired now. When we attack the base at Stella, we'll only have to worry about taking out one helicopter."

"But how do you intend to get past that electric fence and all those armed goons in the barracks?" Alby asked.

"We can't just fly over the fence in a chopper," Calvin James remarked. "Those whirlybirds aren't quiet. The enemy will hear us coming and shoot us out of the sky."

"What about dropping us in the sea and we swim the rest of the way?" Rafael Encizo suggested.

"We'd have to be dropped at least two miles from shore," Manning said. "We'd all be pretty tired by then, except maybe you and Mr. Scott, and we'd still have to get through that electrified fence before we could take out the sentries. Pretty tough to do without attracting attention."

"How about an aircraft that would be silent?" Katz inquired thoughtfully.

"A sailplane," McCarter suggested, smiling. "Of course—we can float right over the fence without making a sound if we use a glider. If it's painted black, they probably won't see us at night until we land right on their bloody airfield."

"That isn't an airfield," Manning reminded him. "It's just a helicopter pad."

"I can land a glider on it," the Briton insisted. "I once landed a twin-engine Beech on a gravel driveway. Remember?"

"Yeah," Encizo growled. "I was in the plane when you did it. Broke off both wings."

"But neither one of us got so much as a scratch," McCarter declared.

"Getting you chaps a glider won't be difficult," Alby assured them. "But, assuming you do sail right into the enemy base, how are you going to take on a small army?"

"Without mercy, Major Alby," Katz replied simply.

18

Security had been reinforced on Stella Island. Several armed men patrolled the estate. Floodlights illuminated the area and lit up the surrounding section beyond the electrified fence. Guards watched the night sky and listened for the ominous thunder of engines.

There was considerable activity inside the main house. Don Fazzio fed dozens of files and records into an incinerator, while Henri LeTrec contacted MERGE headquarters in Paris, France. LeTrec shut off the transatlantic radio and took a code book from his pocket.

"Our destination is Guadeloupe," the Corsican announced. "From there we'll be flown to France. Not directly, of course, but we'll arrive in Europe safely and with all valuables intact."

"Goddamn Ortega," the don growled as he burned the last of his records. "None of this would have happened if that stupid spic hadn't killed Congressman Franklin. Everything turned to shit after that."

"Perhaps," LeTrec said with a shrug. "But for your sake, I hope you can convince the MERGE high command that the failure of the operations in the Bahamas isn't your fault. After all, you were in charge here."

"You know what happened here," Fazzio snapped.

"I'm not really sure," LeTrec replied. "Apparently

the police weren't responsible. Neither was the American CIA. British Secret Service and the Bahamian SIS certainly couldn't do all of these on their own.''

"There's only one type of man who fights the way our enemy fights," Fazzio said grimly. "Until now, I thought there was only one man who could inspire such terror. One man who could strike from any shadow with the destruction of a volcanic eruption.''

"But Mack Bolan is dead, *mon ami*!'' LeTrec exclaimed.

"Yeah?'' the don scoffed. "Maybe he is and maybe he isn't. But whoever we're up against uses the same tactics, and they're just as dangerous. They might even be worse...if that's possible. I lived through two Bolan campaigns. And this has been the same sort of nightmare all over again.''

"Well,'' LeTrec replied, "we're leaving the Bahamas and we'll leave all those boogeymen behind. By the way, is Señor Vargas coming along with us?''

"It was a mistake to let spics into MERGE,'' Fazzio growled. "The Colombian was a screw-up and the Mexican isn't any better. The hell with him.''

"If Vargas is captured,'' LeTrec said, "he might talk.''

"Don't worry about that,'' Fazzio remarked as he yanked open a desk drawer and took out a .38 snubnose revolver. "Vargas won't get a chance to say shit.''

"I hope you remember that you'll need me to get to Europe,'' the Corsican remarked.

"I won't forget,'' Fazzio assured him. "Now let's pack the bonds and cash. Bound to need it for our trip.''

The roar of an explosion outside the house surprised

the gangsters. LeTrec fumbled for a .32 Beretta in his shoulder leather. Fazzio shook his head.

"Forget about shooting your way out of this mess," the don told him, pocketing his own pistol. "Let the men fight the invaders. While they keep the bastards busy, we'll try to slip away."

"Can you fly a helicopter?" LeTrec inquired, reluctantly returning his Beretta to its holster.

"No," Fazzio admitted. "But I can handle a boat well enough. Come on, damn it! It's the only chance we've got."

"All right," the Corsican responded. "Let's go."

PHOENIX FORCE HAD ARRIVED.

A jet-black sailplane had swooped down on the island of Stella like a giant avenging eagle. It knifed through the night sky and sailed over the top of the electrified fence. Sentries glimpsed a huge shadow, silently gliding overhead. No one realized what the object was until it touched down on the helicopter pad.

"Oh, fuck!" a MERGE gunman exclaimed as he worked the bolt of his Thompson submachine gun.

The glider skidded across the surface. A wing struck the Sikorsky helicopter that stood on the pad, the last aircraft in the gangsters' fleet. Plywood and fiberglass cracked on impact. The Sikorsky slid several feet, pushed by the sailplane until David McCarter brought the glider to a full stop.

"Piece of cake," the British pilot announced, undisturbed by the fact the sailplane had pivoted suddenly to ram its nose into the carriage of the unmanned copter. Fortunately the glider did not have a propeller.

"Jesus," Manning muttered. "You sure love to wreck aircraft, David."

"It's what I live for," the Briton replied cheerfully as he kicked open the door to the glider.

Colonel Katzenelenbogen had already burst through another plywood door and jumped onto a wing even before the sailplane had completed its halt. The Israeli hopped to the ground, an M-79 grenade launcher braced across his prosthetic arm and his Uzi slung over a shoulder.

Enemy gunmen charged the twenty-foot Osprey L-22 sailplane. Most gliders are designed to carry only one or two riders, but the Osprey can handle six. Several trigger men searched the skies, fearful of more silent-winged invaders. Others opened fire on the sailplane. Bullets chewed into the frame of the Osprey. Most of the projectiles struck at the tail, hoping to explode a fuel tank that did not exist.

Katz triggered his M-79. The grenade launcher belched, lobbing a 40mm projectile into the center of a cluster of gunmen. The grenade exploded, spewing thermite across the parade field. Liquid fire splashed the hoodlums unlucky enough to survive the initial explosion. They shrieked in agony as they dashed about, clothing aflame, thermite burning through flesh and muscle to sear into bone marrow.

Calvin James leaped from the glider, an M-16 assault rifle in his fists. The black warrior was armed to the teeth. An M-203 grenade launcher was attached to the barrel of his Sixteen, and he carried a pouchful of cartridge grenades on his hip. He also wore his shoulder holster with the Colt Commander in leather and a .357 Smith & Wesson Magnum on his right hip.

While Katz fired a volley of Uzi mercy rounds into the burning victims of his thermite attack, James turned his attention to the northeast where two MERGE hitmen were closing in fast. The black man's M-16 snarled, spitting a thin tongue of flame through a flash-suppressor attached to the muzzle. Copper-jacketed 5.56mm slugs plowed into the enemy troops, shredding chests to burst hearts like blood-filled balloons.

James watched the gunmen fall. Then he jammed the buttstock of the M-16 against his hip and aimed the M-203 at the hangars. The black man triggered the launcher. A grenade sailed to the trio of structures and exploded. Thermite burst across the closest hangar and filled the interior with blazing hell.

Screams blended with the crackle of fire. A lone figure dashed from the hangar, his body draped with dancing flames. James quickly hosed the burning man with 5.56mm rounds to terminate his suffering forever. The fire inside the hangar continued. Fuel supplies were ignited and exploded. The first hangar was torn apart by the blast, and the blaze immediately spread to the second and third structures.

James caught movement via the corner of his right eye. He started to turn to face the new threat, but a killer armed with a Bushmaster machine pistol already had the drop on him. Full-auto flame leaped from the muzzle of McCarter's M-10 Ingram. The thug's skull vanished when half a dozen 9mm parabellums tore through his face. The Bushmaster dropped unfired from twitching, lifeless fingers.

The Briton jumped down from an Osprey wing, the Ingram attached to a shoulder strap, in his right fist, and an H&K 69A1 in his left hand. McCarter also carried his Browning and plenty of extra ammo for his weapons.

McCarter let the Ingram hang by its strap and aimed his Heckler & Koch at the main house. The 69A1 is a compact grenade launcher that resembles an oversize flare pistol, but it still packs a 40mm wallop. McCarter fired the weapon and hurled a grenade shell through a picture window. Shatter resistant or not, the glass gave way under the big projectile and the wide pane burst apart. A merciless thermite charge erupted inside the house, instantly setting a room ablaze—as well as the trio of MERGE gunmen who had been lurking there.

Rafael Encizo headed for the billets, carrying a Sterling submachine gun and an M-79 launcher. Two gun-toting thugs suddenly materialized less than two yards in front of the Cuban battle expert, and four other MERGE troopers were pouring out of the barracks. The hoods were accustomed to taking on inexperienced and generally unarmed opponents. But Encizo was a professional warrior and considered six against one to be fair odds.

The Cuban's Sterling blaster opened fire before the two closest buttonmen could trigger a weapon. A salvo of 115-grain flat-nosed parabellums chopped the MERGE boys into bloody pulp and kicked their bodies backward out of Encizo's path.

The Phoenix combat veteran jammed the butt of his M-79 against his left hip and snap-aimed. He triggered the launcher. A 40mm messenger of devastation sailed into the group of hoods who were rushing to aid their comrades. Instead, they ran straight into hell. Thermite exploded among the gunmen, showering them with liquid brimstone.

Gary Manning was the last man to leave the sailplane.

He carried an M-16 with an M-203 attachment as well as a .41 Magnum revolver and his ever-present pack of assorted explosives. The Canadian demolitions expert lingered by the Sikorsky chopper long enough to clamp a small magnetic Limpet mine to the carriage of the copter. He set the timer and hurried away from the Sikorsky. Thirty seconds later, the Sikorsky erupted in a giant orange-and-black fireball.

Phoenix Force had already planned its strategy of attack. Manning joined Encizo to take care of the barracks. Both men lobbed thermite grenades into the building. The billets immediately burst into an inferno with four walls. MERGE flunkies bolted from the fire, some already human torches drenched in liquid damnation. Others still wielded weapons. None survived.

Manning covered the front entrance while Encizo watched the back. Hoods charged straight into the twin columns of full-auto projectiles that rained the final judgment on every goon who escaped the burning horror inside the barracks.

Katz had told Major Alby the truth.

Phoenix Force attacked without mercy.

WHILE MANNING AND ENCIZO took out the billets, the other three members of Phoenix Force concentrated on the main house. After he destroyed the hangars, Calvin James circled around to the rear of the house. Katz and McCarter attacked from the front.

Although a fire already burned within part of the split-level dwelling, Phoenix Force did not want to burn it to the ground. The leaders of the Bahamian MERGE operations would be more valuable alive than dead. If they failed to take any prisoners, the house still offered the greatest possibility of information concerning other MERGE activities.

Katz loaded an HE grenade in the breech of his M-79 and fired it at the front door of the house. The explosive smashed the heavy oak door off its hinges. David McCarter rushed to the ragged entrance and tossed an SAS "flash-bang" grenade across the threshold. He raised the Ingram machine pistol, opened his mouth and waited.

The grenade did not explode.

"Bloody dud," the Briton decided as he dived through the doorway.

McCarter hit the floor in a rapid shoulder roll and came up on one knee, the M-10 in his fists. A polished shoe lashed out and suddenly kicked the Ingram from the Briton's hands. McCarter lost his balance and fell on his back. The muzzle of a Thompson submachine gun stared back at the commando's face.

Instinct and reflexes took over. McCarter swatted the barrel of the subgun, catching it and shoving the Tommy away from his head. His boot rose swiftly, delivering a steel-toed kick between his opponent's splayed legs. The hoodlum assailant bellowed with pain as he triggered his Thompson. A volley of .45 projectiles ripped into a wall as McCarter continued to hold the barrel away from his face.

Twisting hard, McCarter pulled his opponent off balance and tripped him with a kick to an ankle. The thug crashed to the floor beside McCarter. The Briton quickly mounted his foe and shoved his left hand against the frame of the Thompson, pinning the gun to the guy's chest. McCarter's right hand lashed twice, karate-chopping the gunman across the temple. He delivered a *lung tao* punch to the sphenoid bone, his knuckles driving skull fragments into his attacker's brain.

The roar of an automatic weapon filled the hallway. McCarter glanced up to see the bullet-riddled body of a MERGE gunman hurtle backward into a wall. The man fell dead, hands locked around the frame of a sawed-off shotgun. Yakov Katzenelenbogen gazed down at McCarter. A whisp of smoke rose from the barrel of the Israeli's Uzi.

"Next time," Katz told him, "lob another grenade before you charge inside."

"Thanks," McCarter replied with a grin as he gathered up his Ingram. "Next time I will."

Katz moved up the hallway, followed by McCarter. Both men stayed close to the wall and remained alert to possible danger. The house was gradually filling up with smoke. Two MERGE underlings stumbled toward the Phoenix Force pair. Both men held their hands on top of their heads as they staggered from a dense gray cloud.

"Shit, man!" one of them cried. "We give up!"

Katz held his fire and told the pair to keep their hands up and come forward. The men obeyed and moved closer on unsteady legs. McCarter held the Ingram M-10 in one hand as he fished two riot cuffs from a pouch on his belt.

"Didn't think we'd get any of these blokes alive," the Briton mused.

"Where's Fazzio?" Katz demanded.

"Office is over there," one of the thugs replied as he lowered an arm to point down the corridor.

Suddenly he grabbed Katz's Uzi and yanked it from the Israeli's hand. The guy jumped back and fumbled for the trigger as he tried to point the chatterbox at McCarter. The Briton fired his Ingram, and the top of the hoodlum's skull was blown away by three 9mm rounds just above the forehead.

The other thug had tried to jump Katz. He swung a five-inch blade at the Israeli's face. Yakov weaved out of the path of the blade and raised his prosthesis as the knife artist lunged for his throat. The tri-hook at the end of Katz's artificial arm snapped together. The hood gasped when he realized the blade of his knife was trapped in the three hooks.

Katz rapidly drew his SIG-Sauer autoloader with his left hand and thumbed off the ambidextrous safety. The Israeli jammed the P-226 pistol under the guy's extended arm and fired a 9mm parabellum into the armpit. The terrific shock to the nerve center located in that sensitive area rendered the thug unconscious. He fell to the floor and began to bleed to death.

Yakov holstered his pistol and gathered up the Uzi while McCarter took the point. The Briton led the way through the hall, Katz following to guard the rear. McCarter stopped and pointed to a door. Katz nodded.

The Briton aimed his M-10 and fired a 3-round burst. Splinters jutted from the door above and beside the lock. The door swayed open, the lock shattered. Then a bullet smashed through the top panel and buried itself in a wall.

McCarter advanced quickly, firing another volley through the panels as he ran and quickly jumped to the side of the door. It creaked open. McCarter nudged it with the back of his heel and it swung back again. Katz poked the barrel of his Uzi through the gap and sprayed the room beyond with 9mm hail.

A man screamed and a body thudded against the floor. Katz entered, barely glancing at the bullet-torn body on the carpet. The Israeli was more interested in the man at the opposite end of a long conference table.

Juan Vargas was desperate. The Mexican Mafia boss

had found himself trapped in the conference room with only one personal bodyguard, who now lay dead on the floor. There seemed to be only one route to escape. Vargas had smashed a window near the piranha tank. He shoved a chair to the wall and prepared to climb over the sill when Katz entered.

The Israeli fired a short, 3-round blast. Nine-millimeter slugs slashed into the Mexican's legs. Vargas cried out and fell from the chair. He landed headfirst against the top of the aquarium. Glass cracked and the lid gave way.

The piranha swarmed over Vargas's head. Razor teeth ripped flesh. Jaws gulped meat greedily and bit again and again. Blood poured from gouged-out eye sockets and the water turned crimson. Katz rushed to the aquarium and used his hook to pull Juan Vargas from the tank.

"Oh, God," the Israeli whispered when he gazed down at the tattered remnants of the man's face.

Katz had seen much horror and brutality in his life, but he was not immune to disgust or pity. Vargas's face was little more than a skull draped with shreds of chewed flesh and torn muscles. A piranha clung to his throat, teeth buried in a carotid. Katz aimed the Uzi at that hideous face—a face he would see again and again in future nightmares.

He squeezed the trigger.

"Yakov?" McCarter began as he approached. "You all right?"

"Yeah," Katz replied woodenly. "I'm all right. Let's go see how the others are doing."

"Oh, shit," McCarter rasped when he glimpsed the corpse of Juan Vargas. The piranha flopped about on the carpet near the shattered head.

"One that didn't get away," the Israeli said grimly.

"Don't shoot, guys," a familiar voice urged. "It's Cal."

McCarter and Katz turned to see Calvin James at the doorway. The black commando canted his M-16 over a shoulder as he entered the room. His relaxed manner suggested the battle was over, but tension in his face revealed that their work was not yet over.

"Gary and Rafael have taken care of the billets," James announced. "A couple of dudes were hiding in a ditch. They came out with their hands up and surrendered. I think they're all the prisoners we've got."

"They'll have to do," Katz replied.

"But I just saw a speedboat cut out for the Sound," James added quickly. "I don't know if anybody important is getting away or not. Figure we should follow 'em?"

"How's the glider, David?" Katz asked the Briton.

"Nothing that three days of repairs and alterations can't fix," McCarter answered. "Unless Gary blew up the helicopter next to it."

"He did." James confirmed. "The glider is totaled, man. But maybe there's another boat."

"You and Rafael are best qualified to go after these runaways," Katz declared. "The rest of us will mop up here and check for anyone who may have crawled under a rock."

"Okay," James agreed eagerly. "Good luck."

"Good hunting," McCarter replied.

19

Rafael Encizo piloted the eight-foot speedboat while Calvin James bailed water from the deck. They had already set out to sea before they discovered the leak. Someone had put a bullet through the fiberglass hull of the boat.

"We're not doing real well here, amigo," the Cuban warned as he checked the fuel gauge. "If we don't catch up with the bastards in another five minutes, I'm turning us around and heading back to Stella Island."

"I don't believe you," James said, scooping up more water and tossing it over the side. "A moonlight cruise in the Bahamas and you're bitchin' about a little thing like a leaky boat."

"Well," Encizo sighed. "Besides the leak, we're running low on fuel and the oil pressure doesn't look good, either. And no offense, but you're not my idea of romantic company, Calvin."

"Guess I can live with that," the black man commented dryly. "Figure there are any sharks in these waters?"

"I don't want to find out," Encizo replied. "Hey, I see something up ahead."

In the distance, a white-and-blue speedboat was cutting across the waves. The Cuban steered the Phoenix

Force vessel toward the fleeing craft and pushed the throttles forward. James gathered up his M-16.

"Can we catch up?" he asked.

"The leak is slowing us down," Encizo stated, a trace of frustration in his voice. "And our quarry obviously took the best boat for himself."

"Try to get close enough for me to get an accurate shot," James urged. "Maybe we can slow them down, too."

"I'm doing the best I can," the Cuban insisted.

But the fleeing MERGE members had noticed they were being pursued. The enemy vessel accelerated and bolted farther ahead. Encizo shook his head with dismay. The chase was hopeless.

Suddenly two larger boats appeared along the velvet horizon. The MERGE craft tried to steer around them, but one of the vessels quickly swung into the path of the speedboat, forcing it to retreat.

"This is Coastal Patrol," a voice bellowed from a bullhorn. "You are ordered to stop and allow yourselves to be boarded."

"I am Major Alby of the Security Intelligence Service," a familiar voice added from another loudspeaker. "We must insist that you stop for questioning. Criminals are suspected of being in these waters. If you are innocent, you have nothing to fear. However, if you refuse to cooperate...."

The enemy vessel made a desperate dash to the southeast. A .50-caliber machine gun snarled from the deck of one of the patrol boats. Tracer rounds lit up the night sky as a salvo was fired over the heads of the two men in the MERGE craft.

"Next time we'll blow you out of the water," Alby warned.

The boat containing Calvin James and Rafael Encizo slowly drew closer. The Phoenix Force pair saw the men aboard the enemy speedboat. They did not recognize either Don Antonio Fazzio or Henri LeTrec, but both MERGE leaders had the prosperous, decorated-garbage-can look of big-time mobsters.

Floodlights from the patrol vessels lit up a quarter-mile radius. The gangsters' boat seemed trapped by the light as it circled around and around like a caged beast.

"Stop the boat," LeTrec said urgently. "There's no way we can escape."

"Don't be an asshole," Fazzio growled, turning the wheel and shifting the throttles. "I've got some diving gear in a transom box. Get it out."

"Are you mad!" the Corsican exclaimed. "You can't swim out here!"

"Just get it and quit whining, you frog shithead," the don snapped, talking like the product of gutters that he truly was.

Fazzio steered the boat with one hand as he awkwardly stripped off his white silk shirt. The don's muscles bulged as he struggled to accomplish both tasks at the same time. Fazzio was in excellent physical condition, and LeTrec was dreadfully out of shape. But this did not worry the Corsican as he drew his Beretta pistol and aimed it at the back of Fazzio's head.

"Stop the boat or I'll kill you," he said simply. "And no tricks, Fazzio."

"You're full of surprises, Henri," the don muttered, but he shut off the engine. "Happy?"

"Take your gun out and toss it overboard," the Corsican instructed. "Careful, *mon ami*. I will not hesitate to kill you if you force my hand."

"I believe you," Fazzio assured him.

The don used two fingers to draw his .38 revolver and carefully hurl it into the sea. LeTrec then tossed his own Beretta overboard and held up his hands for the patrol to see.

Fazzio suddenly pulled a Mark II diver's knife from an ankle sheath. He whirled and rose from behind the wheel to thrust the five-inch blade into LeTrec's stomach. LeTrec screamed as Fazzio shoved the wounded Corsican to the deck. He stabbed LeTrec again, driving the knife between the ribs.

"Looks like those guys had a difference of opinion," Calvin James remarked. "But the dude with the knife sure got his point across."

"What does he think he's going to do now?" Encizo wondered aloud.

They watched Fazzio crawl to the transom box. He opened it and removed a pair of swim fins, diver's face mask and an air tank with regulator. He tossed the flippers and tank overboard.

"Crazy bastard," James hissed as he unbuckled his gunbelt. "He's gonna try to swim for it."

"We could just shoot him," Encizo remarked, slipping off his shoulder holster.

"Let's try to take him alive," James replied as he opened the transom box to see what supplies they carried. "Shit. All we've got is one mask."

Fazzio dived over the side of his boat. The don expertly grabbed his tank and pulled it underwater. James quickly unlaced his boots. A rifle shot cracked from one of the patrol boats. Alby's voice boomed from a bullhorn, ordering the men to hold their fire.

"Forget it, Cal," Encizo urged. "Let the patrol flush him out."

"You just keep them from firing into the water," James told him as he stripped off his shirt.

"Hold on, Cal," Encizo warned. "That creep has an air tank and flippers. That means he can stay underwater without having to come up to breathe. He'll also be able to move in the water better with fins on."

"Yeah," the black man commented as he pulled on the diving mask. "They taught me that when I was in the SEALs. But if I can get the bastard and cut his air hose, then he'll have to come up. Right?"

"If he doesn't cut your belly open first," the Cuban cautioned his partner. He handed James his Cold Steel Tanto. "This is better suited for underwater combat than your Jet-Aer dagger."

"Thanks," James said as he accepted the knife.

The black warrior hopped over the side. The water was cold, chilled by the night, but the floodlights created a glow across the surface. An assortment of colorful tropical fish swam all around James as he paddled his arms and legs gently. Water plants waved from the bottom. Something large moved suddenly beneath James. He rotated his body to get a better look, Tanto held ready for action.

A great barracuda cut through the water. It was almost seven feet long, larger than many sharks that have attacked divers. The barracuda can be dangerous, but, like sharks, they do not generally try to make a meal of humans. However, barracuda are unpredictable. James watched the big fish circle about, probably confused by the floodlights above.

Without warning, Don Fazzio struck. The gangster seemed to materialize from nowhere. He had managed to slip into the harness of his air tank and put on his flippers. The don took advantage of the barracuda distraction to close in rapidly, his Mark II in his fist.

The blade raked James's forearm. Blood curled like ink in the water and the Tanto slipped from the Phoenix fighter's grasp. Fazzio's eyes narrowed behind the lens of his face mask as he thrust the Mark II toward James's belly.

The black commando's left hand grabbed Fazzio's wrist as his right reached for the mouthpiece between the gangster's teeth. Fighting underwater is frustrating because it reduces movement and slows attacking limbs. Fazzio seized James's arm and the pair pivoted in a macabre water ballet.

James broke free of Fazzio's grip and used both hands to wrench the wrist above the Mark II. The don's fingers opened and his knife drifted toward the bottom. However, Fazzio's free hand pulled James's head back as he maneuvered himself behind the black man.

Fazzio wrapped an arm around James's neck, applying a rear choke hold. His forearm pressed against the commando's throat while the hard biceps muscle jammed into the side of his neck. James's lungs felt as if they were about to burst from his chest. Painful lights popped inside his head. Both men sunk deeper. Farther from life-sustaining air above.

James pulled at the crook of his opponent's elbow to ease the pressure at his throat. The Phoenix pro's other hand reached back and clawed at Fazzio's face. His fingers caught the rim of the gangster's mask. James shoved hard and felt the face mask give way.

The mask slipped from Fazzio's face. Saltwater stung his eyes, startling the don. James dug an elbow into his opponent's ribs and pulled the choking arm to slip loose. His lungs ached and his head seemed mired in quicksand as he turned in the water to face Fazzio.

James grabbed the mouthpiece and shoved his other hand against the don's forehead. The mouthpiece popped loose from Fazzio's teeth. James quickly stuck the device in his own mouth. He breathed deeply, forcing himself not to gulp air too fast.

Fazzio reached for the hose. James grabbed both his elbows and pushed hard to keep the man's hands away from the mouthpiece. The commando suddenly kicked his feet outward and wrapped a scissors hold around Fazzio's waist. James locked his ankles, squeezing his legs under the don's ribs, applying pressure under Fazzio's lungs and diaphragm. The men sunk faster, deeper. James continued to breathe steadily through the air hose as he held his opponent at bay.

James felt Fazzio struggle with the strength and fury of desperation. The black crusader held on and rode Fazzio to the sandy bottom. When they touched down, the don no longer struggled. Fazzio's mouth hung open, his eyes staring lifelessly back at Calvin James. Don Antonio Fazzio had drowned.

MAJOR ALBY AND RAFAEL ENCIZO helped Calvin James climb aboard the patrol boat. The black man had left the corpse of Don Fazzio at the bottom of the ocean. He unbuckled the confiscated air tank from his back, happy to be rid of the dead man's diving gear. Alby offered him a cup of hot tea. James hated tea, but at that moment it tasted better than champagne.

"Are you all right, Mr. Scott?" Alby inquired.

"Who?" James replied. "Oh, yeah. I'm okay. Sure was a waste of time trying to take that dude alive, though."

"That dude was Don Fazzio," Encizo announced. "The fellow he knifed lived long enough to name his assassin. We'd better get back to Stella Island and let the others know how everything turned out."

"Thank God it's over," Alby declared with a sigh of relief.

"Our mission is over and MERGE operations in the Bahamas have come to an end for now," James said wearily. "But MERGE is international and it's been growing in the shadows like a fungus for the last couple of years. We can't let it go unchecked any longer."

"You're right, amigo," Encizo agreed grimly. "We haven't seen the last of MERGE. This was just the beginning."

Mack Bolan's

PHOENIX FORCE

by Gar Wilson

Schooled in guerrilla warfare, equipped with all the latest lethal hardware, Phoenix Force battles the powers of darkness in an endless crusade for freedom, justice and the rights of the individual. Follow the adventures of one of the legends of the genre. Phoenix Force is the free world's foreign legion!

"Gar Wilson is excellent! Raw action attacks the reader on every page."

—*Don Pendleton*

Phoenix Force titles are available wherever paperbacks are sold.

GOLD EAGLE

Mack Bolan's

ABLE TEAM

by Dick Stivers

Action writhes in the reader's own street as Able Team's Carl "Mr. Ironman" Lyons, Pol Blancanales and Gadgets Schwarz make triple trouble in blazing war. To these superspecialists, justice is as sharp as a knife. Join the guys who began it all—Dick Stivers's Able Team!

"This guy has a fertile mind and a great eye for detail. Dick Stivers is brilliant!"

—*Don Pendleton*

Able Team titles are available wherever paperbacks are sold.

GOLD EAGLE

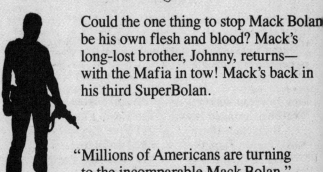

GET THE NEW WAR BOOK AND MACK BOLAN BUMPER STICKER FREE!

Mail this coupon today!

FREE! THE NEW WAR BOOK AND MACK BOLAN BUMPER STICKER
when you join our home subscription plan.

Gold Eagle Reader Service, a division of Worldwide Library
In U.S.A.: 2504 W. Southern Avenue, Tempe, Arizona 85282
In Canada: P.O. Box 2800, Postal Station A, 5170 Yonge Street, Willowdale, Ont. M2N 6J3

YES, rush me The New War Book and Mack Bolan bumper sticker FREE, and, under separate cover, my first six Gold Eagle novels. These first six books are mine to examine free for 10 days. If I am not entirely satisfied with these books, I will return them within 10 days and owe nothing. If I decide to keep these novels, I will pay just $1.95 per book (total $11.70). I will then receive the six Gold Eagle novels every other month, and will be billed the same low price of $11.70 per shipment. I understand that each shipment will contain two Mack Bolan novels, and one each from the Able Team, Phoenix Force, SOBs and Track libraries. There are no shipping and handling or any other hidden charges. I may cancel this arrangement at any time, and The New War Book and bumper sticker are mine to keep as gifts, even if I do not buy any additional books.

IMPORTANT BONUS: If I continue to be an active subscriber to Gold Eagle Reader Service, you will send me FREE, with every shipment, the AUTOMAG newsletter as a FREE BONUS!

Name	(please print)	
Address		Apt. No.
City	State/Province	Zip/Postal Code
Signature	(If under 18, parent or guardian must sign.)	

This offer limited to one order per household. We reserve the right to exercise discretion in granting membership. If price changes are necessary you will be notified.

116-BPM-PAE5

AA-SUB-1R

Mack Bolan is a Winner!

Readers everywhere applaud his success.

"You deserve some kind of reward for delivering such reading pleasure to millions of people throughout the world."

M.L., Chicago, Illinois

"Bolan isn't a killer—he is a positive force fighting the degeneration of man. He is also awesomely entertaining, as fine a literary hero as any."

S.S., Augsburg, Germany

"I want to congratulate you on your decision to put our Sergeant into the fight against terrorism. With the world situation today, it will endear many more people to this man of courage."

B.C., New York, New York

"I am in the army, and I would be proud to serve with Mack Bolan and cover his back down the first mile, and second, and third if he said it was needed."

P.E.D., APO, New York

"I think my Executioner collection is the finest thing I own, or probably ever will own."

R.C., Gainesville, Florida

Names available on request.